GIRLS CAN VLOG

Festival Frenzy

'Pitch-perfect fiction for the new digital generation' *Lancashire Evening Post*

'Funny and inspirational story about the world of vlogging' *Bookseller*

'Warm, funny, and perfect for the Zoella generation, this series is bang on trend and sure to be a hit' *The Mile Long Bookshelf*

'A really fun read . . . sends out a really positive message that social networking can be a powerful force for good when it's supported by a healthy dose of interaction in the real world' Sugarscape

'Makes great reading for anyone who wants to give vlogging a go' *Week Junior*

'The story itself is wonderful, funny and descriptive – so much so that I read the whole thing in one day!' Ella, age 11, a Lovereading4kids.co.uk Reader Review Panel member

'I really enjoyed this funny book' Miyah, age 10, a Lovereading4kids.co.uk Reader Review Panel member·

'A brilliant story about friends, vlogging and adorable animals!' Sidr̶ ̶ ̶ ̶ ̶ ̶ ̶ ̶ ̶ ̶ ̶ ̶kids.co.uk Read̶ ̶ ̶

Books by Emma Moss

The Girls Can Vlog series

Lucy Locket: Online Disaster

Amazing Abby: Drama Queen

Hashtag Hermione: Wipeout!

Jazzy Jessie: Going for Gold

Emma Moss

GIRLS CAN VLOG

Festival Frenzy!

MACMILLAN CHILDREN'S BOOKS

First published 2018 by Macmillan Children's Books
an imprint of Pan Macmillan
20 New Wharf Road, London N1 9RR
Associated companies throughout the world
www.panmacmillan.com

ISBN 978-1-5098-8536-7

Based on an original concept by Ingrid Selberg
Copyright © Ingrid Selberg Consulting Limited and Emma Young 2018

The right of Ingrid Selberg and Emma Young to be identified as the
authors of this work has been asserted by them in
accordance with the Copyright, Designs and Patents Act 1988.

1 3 5 7 9 8 6 4 2

A CIP catalogue record for this book is available from
the British Library.

Design by The Dimpse
Printed and bound by CPI Group (UK) Ltd, Croydon CR0 4YY

For George and Lauren, Harry Potter expert advisers x

Chapter One: Lucy

To: morgan_lives_here@hotmail.com

From: lucylocket@freemail.co.uk

Hey, Morgan!

How are you? Enjoying that California sunshine, I bet . . . I SO ENVY YOU! We had, like, three days of sun but now it's pouring with rain and so cold I'm wearing tracksuit bottoms and a hoody. It's supposed to be summer. ☂

School's out – finally – but I'm sooo bummed out that I can't come to visit you after all. Mom and Dad said it was just too expensive ☹ and also they want me to help babysit Maggie as they are both really busy. I know I shouldn't complain – at least they both have jobs . . . I've seen how tough it is for Jessie's family with her dad out of work.

ANYWAY . . . I NEED TO STOP WHINING!

Summer will be great – outside of babysitting, I'll have loads of time to hang out with the Girls Can Vlog gang, who are almost as much fun as you😃and come up with some creative new vlogs. Plus I'll get to see a lot of Sam ❤❤❤ at the farm – he keeps moaning that I don't have time for him any more.

So loads to look forward to – maybe there will be some surprises too! I hope you also have some amazing things planned – but nothing as amazing as seeing yours truly, as that is impossible hahahaha.

Loads of love from your frozen bestie,

LUCY XOXO

Lucy pressed send and sighed. She was really disappointed not to be able to visit her best friend, Morgan, and catch up with all her old friends in America. Sometimes she missed her former life, but at least she had a brilliant new gang now – Abby, Hermione and Jessie – and their Girls Can Vlog YouTube channel was growing in leaps and bounds. This summer they'd have lots of free time for filming and incorporating their new member Sassy's ideas into the videos. And then there was Lucy's gorgeous boyfriend, Sam . . . whom she would have missed massively if she'd gone away.

'Lucy! Dinner! Now!' her mum called from downstairs.

It smelt like stirfry, and Lucy was hungry, so she hurried on down. Foghorn, her fluffy grey cat, streaked down the stairs too, hoping for a kitty pouch – though Lucy's mum had put him on a strict diet.

When everyone was seated at the table, Mrs Lockwood announced, 'So about this summer . . .'

Lucy rolled her eyes. 'I know, I know. I can't go to the US. And I have to babysit Mags.' She grinned at her four-year-old sister. 'C-could be worse, but we're only watching *Frozen* once a day, K?'

Maggie rolled her eyes too. 'I hate *Frozen*,' she announced. 'My favourite film is *Moana*.'

Lucy giggled – this was news to her. But that was her sister all over: always unpredictable and always hilarious.

'Lucyloo, I know you're very disappointed about the trip to America,' said her father, stroking Foghorn as he begged for food, 'but your mother and I have some news that should cheer you up.'

Lucy looked up curiously. 'News?'

'Yes,' announced her mother. 'We know it's not America, but we thought it would be fun to have a family camping trip.'

'Camping?' shrieked Maggie in delight. 'Sleeping outside? In tents?'

'Exactly,' said Mr Lockwood. 'Tents, sleeping bags, campfires, toasted marshmallows. The whole shebang . . . fresh air and nature. I can't wait! I was once a Boy Scout, you know . . .'

'Yes, Dad, we know.' Lucy sighed; she'd heard the stories before. 'That's pretty cool. We haven't been on a trip in ages.' But Lucy had mixed feelings about spending a whole week with her family, trapped in a tent. She looked out of the window, the rain hammering against the glass. Trading sunny California for a soggy tent didn't seem overly appealing.

'There's more,' said her mum with a smile. 'We'll be renting a campervan, so there will be some spare seats. I thought you might like to invite some of your friends to join us, Lucy. Would you like that?'

Lucy's mixed feelings suddenly weren't so mixed.

'M-my friends could come too?' she asked, her stammer intensified by her excitement. 'R-really? That would b-be sooo amaaazing! Oh, Mom, thank you, thank you.' She leaped up and gave her mother a hug. 'H-how many?' she asked, and held her breath.

How would she choose? There was the cute, nerdy Hermione, who'd befriended her on that horrific first day at school – never to be forgotten – and remained loyal throughout. Hermione wasn't exactly outdoorsy, her accident on the school ski trip had proved that, but she would still enjoy it. Then there was Abby: upbeat, happy, a bit out of control sometimes, but loads of fun. She was a must for the trip to be a success. Plus, she was chairperson of the GCV channel and always bursting with ideas. Prank-loving Jessie was the most outdoorsy of the girls and probably would be the best at all the camping stuff. Finally there was the pink-haired Sassy, who'd recently joined the group . . .

'I think the campervan has seven seats,' said her dad, 'so you can bring three friends. I bet I can guess which three!'

'That's insane! I c-can't wait to tell them! They'll be so excited! I hope they c-can all come.' Lucy pushed the thought of Sassy to the back of her mind – the other three had to come first.

'And now for the EXTRA-good bit,' said Lucy's mum mysteriously as she dished out more of the stirfry. 'As part of the trip, we're going to spend a day at Chesterbury.'

'As in th-the festival?' gasped Lucy.

'Yes,' said Mrs Lockwood. 'We haven't been to a decent music festival since Maggie was born, and you deserve a treat after doing so well this year, settling into your new school.'

Lucy squealed, then reached over and gave her mum a hug.

'It's not the same as a whole summer with Morgan, I know,' added Mrs Lockwood, 'but we thought you'd like it.'

Lucy looked at her incredulously. 'Are you k-kidding? It's Chesterbury – of course I'll like it! I've always wanted to go.' Something occurred to her. 'Can the girls come t-too?' she asked, holding her breath.

'Yes, that's part of the treat!' said her mother. 'My friend helps organize the festival and got me a discount on tickets.'

'Whoop!' cried Lucy. Her parents were the actual best sometimes.

'Your mom is dying to dig out some of her old boho

gear – watch out!' Lucy's dad laughed.

'What's boho?' asked Maggie, picking up a noodle.

Mrs Lockwood laughed. 'A groovy fashion look. Now eat up, everyone, before this food gets stone cold. And sorry, Foghorn, you are out of luck!'

After dinner, lounging in her bedroom, Lucy didn't know who to tell her news first, so she WhatsApped the girls on the group chat – the old one that didn't include Sassy.

20:27

Lucy: Omgggg, guys! Exciting news!

20:27

Abby: What????????

20:27

Lucy: My parents are inviting you all on a camping trip with us . . . and on the last day we're going to Chesterbury!

20:28

Abby: Chesterbury Festival? Seriously???!!!

20:29

Lucy: Seriously! Can you believe it???

20:29

Jessie: Sorry, guys, is this a joke?

20:30

Lucy: NO! They told me to bring three friends. ☺ ☺ ☺

20:33

Hermione: Wow, that's so generous of them . . . Not sure about the camping though . . . think of the INSECTS 😲

20:35

Lucy: H, you'll be fine ☺

20:35

Lucy: My parents are ringing all of your parents RIGHT NOW!

20:40

Jessie: Amazing! I love camping! Ghost stories round the campfire, toasting marshmallows . . . like in all the horror movies! Mwah-ha-ha!

20:41

Abby: Er, guys! Focus on the festival! Ollie Storm is headlining this year I think . . .

20:41

Lucy: YESSS! I just looked it up and you're right! Love him!

20:48

Abby: And think about the amazing vlogs we can do! Hey, what about Sassy?

20:53

Lucy: Not enough room in the van, sadly 😞

20:53

Abby: Aw, that sucks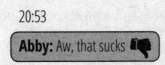

20:56

Lucy: Yeah . . . anyway, talk to your parents and we can meet up tomorrow to start planning?

20:56

Abby: And shopping!

20:59

Jessie: This is so awesome!

21:03

> **Hermione:** Hope I can come xx

The following day, they met up at the cafe in the park. The rain had cleared, so they sat outside having ice cream and enjoying the sun, though it was still chilly. Lucy felt a tiny bit guilty for not inviting Sassy to the park, but there didn't seem to be much point, and it would be hard for her to hear about their camping plans.

Hermione was explaining to Lucy that her mum hadn't been sure about letting her come, but that Hermione's dad had convinced her, saying that she would learn a lot about nature on the trip.

'So I can come,' said Hermione, 'which I am pleased about, but I'm still a bit anxious about sleeping outside. Insects are so disgusting . . . They could just crawl into the tent and on to our faces when we're asleep.'

Lucy laughed, watching her friend grimace at the thought.

'I don't want to learn about nature close up!' Hermione shuddered.

'These things are always scarier in your imagination,' said Lucy soothingly. She often felt protective of Hermione, who had a tendency to worry about things that hadn't happened yet and might never happen. 'D-don't sweat it, H! We'll look after you.'

'Well, I can't wait!' said Jessie, holding her head upside down to catch a drip leaking from her cone. She spoke with her mouth half open. 'The great outdoors . . . So much fresh air, so many opportunities for pranks!'

Abby rushed up last, wearing a blush-pink crop top, shorts and huge new sunglasses, with her cream pug, Weenie, trotting along at her side.

'You l-look cute,' said Lucy, 'even if you are covered in g-goosebumps!' While she was happiest in jeans and the same old comfy T-shirts, she had to admire Abby's firm commitment to fashion.

'Mind over matter!' quipped Abby, rubbing her arms. 'Anyway, we have much more important things to talk about. Such as, what vlogging are we going to do while we're there – and how are we going to prepare for Chesterbury? Has anyone been to a festival before?'

'Nope,' said Lucy and Hermione together.

'Me neither,' said Jessie, 'which is why this whole thing is so hashtag *incredible*!'

'I wonder if Sassy has,' Abby said. 'Seems like the kind of thing she'd have done . . . she loves her music. Down, Weenie! So, Sassy definitely can't come?'

Lucy shook her head.

'It's just such a shame,' said Abby sadly.

Lucy started to feel annoyed. It was going to be an amazing trip, so why was Abby complaining? 'Not enough seats in the v-van, Abs, like I said. So it could only be the four of us. Still pretty c-cool, though, huh?'

'Does it have to be –' Abby broke off and cleared her throat – 'us four? As opposed to, like, three of us and Sassy if one of us can't make it?' She lifted her sunglasses and glanced quickly at Jessie. 'Like, if we have . . . commitments or something.'

Lucy sighed. Abby implying that Jessie wasn't fully

dedicated to the group was becoming a regular thing, and she was getting sick of it.

'We *can* all come,' said Jessie angrily, glaring back at Abby. 'As we just established. So what are you suggesting?'

'Nothing,' said Abby. 'It's just – like – well, I thought you might have had a gymnastics competition or something.'

Lucy saw a hurt look cross Jessie's face and wondered why Abby had to be so insensitive. Just because Jessie had messed up a GCV fashion shoot because of gym one time. She hadn't done it on purpose, and, anyway, that was weeks ago now!

'It's fine – there's less training over the summer,' said Jessie, her tone frostier than her double-choc ice cream, 'but, if you'd prefer Sassy to go in my place, just say.'

'Of course not,' said Hermione anxiously. 'We want you! Don't we, Abs?'

Abby yawned, and Lucy felt herself get angrier. Why wasn't Abby answering? 'D-don't we, Abs?' she prompted, putting her arms round Jessie.

There was a pause and Weenie whined, as if even he could sense the awkward tension in the air.

'Of course,' said Abby eventually, lowering her sunglasses again. 'But we'll have to think of how to let Sassy down gently. We don't want her to get upset.'

'I'll explain,' said Lucy. 'I'm sure she'll understand. W-we haven't been friends for very long, whereas *we've* all known each other for a year at least.' She stared meaningfully at Abby.

'Cool,' said Abby with a shrug. 'Well, let's get down to business. We need to go shopping for our festival gear.'

'The festival's only one day,' said Jessie. 'Most of the time we'll be camping, which means hiking, swimming, canoeing and stuff like that. So we'll need waterproofs and warm hoodies, socks and hiking boots.'

'I suppose . . .' said Abby grudgingly. 'But bikinis as well!'

Lucy had to laugh.

Then Hermione said, 'I don't have a sleeping bag,

so I guess I'll need to get one. Shall we all go into town tomorrow?'

'Yeah. I'll help you choose, H,' said Jessie, 'though I'll be in a smelly old sleeping bag that belonged to my brother, Leon. It can practically walk by itself . . .'

'Eeugh!' said Lucy. 'TMI.'

'Oh, and we need to get like a million delicious snacks for midnight feasts!' exclaimed Jessie. 'I really want to try those new pigs-in-blankets-flavoured crisps.'

Lucy smiled, relieved to see that Abby's weirdness seemed to have been forgotten.

Later that night Lucy was cuddled up in bed with Foghorn, on WhatsApp.

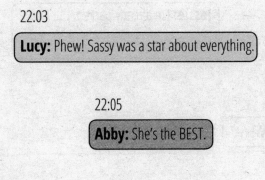

22:03

Lucy: Phew! Sassy was a star about everything.

22:05

Abby: She's the BEST.

22:11

Hermione: So . . . has everyone starting packing?

22:11

Abby: I'm struggling. Think I need a bigger suitcase!

22:13

Lucy: Sorry to break it to you but don't think there's room in the van for suitcases – rucksacks only!

22:13

Abby: 😮

22:16

Jessie: I'm already packed, but I have non-great news . . .

22:17

Lucy: Oh no WHAAT?

22:17

Abby: Spill!

22:19

Jessie: It's about you-know-who!

22:20

Lucy: Not Dakota?

22:21

Jessie: Yep! She's just been gloating online about how she's going to Chesterbury and her dad bought her VIP everything! 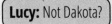 She's probably got a pass to a special VIP Portaloo!

22:23

Abby: I swear that girl only exists to ruin my life! Now the whole festival is spoilt!

22:23

Lucy: Not true!! We're gonna have a great time whatevs.

22:24

Jessie: Roger that!

22:26

Hermione: You've never let her beat you at anything, Abs! Don't start now!

22:28

Abby: True! This festival's gonna be insane! See ya tomorrow, gotta go upload our vlog, Luce xxx

VLOG 1

FADE IN: ABBY'S FAMILY ROOM – EVENING.

ABBY and LUCY on the sofa surrounded by shopping bags. WEENIE peeking out from under bags.

ABBY

Hi, everybody!

LUCY

Hey!

ABBY and LUCY wave.

ABBY

We're just back from a mega-
successful shopping trip. Some of this
stuff we'll show you properly in later vlogs – we'll just give
you a sneak preview for now. So, first, I've been stocking up
on essentials for creating my festival look for Chesterbury. I got
this brilliant eyeshadow palette . . .

ABBY holds it up to the camera.

ABBY (CONTINUED)

and a whole load of glitter make-
up, which I'll be showing you
how to use in a tutorial.

LUCY

Loving the g-glitter, Abs – so pretty! Personally I think I'm
g-gonna stick to denim shorts and vintage T-shirts.

LUCY rummages in her bag.

LUCY (CONTINUED)

My big splurge is this pair of
awesome t-trainers. I love them so
much, I'm gonna take them to bed
with me tonight.

They laugh.

ABBY

Let's just hope it doesn't rain at Chesterbury –
they won't stay that lovely lilac for long if it's muddy!

JOSH and CHARLIE enter the room, grab some snacks and slump
down on the sofas.

JOSH

(looks around)

Did you leave anything in the shops?

ABBY

(defensive)

Honestly, I didn't buy that much . . . It's all essentials . . . and Chesterbury is ALL about fashion.

JOSH

Really? I thought it was about music. Silly me.

ABBY

Not funny! And don't eat all the tortilla chips, Josh!

CHARLIE waves to the camera.

CHARLIE

Hi, GCV viewers! Me and Josh will be there too, doing some

Prankingstein Live from the festival. We've come up with some really sick challenges to do there.

JOSH

Yeah, one idea is the Lipgloss Challenge, where you put on different flavoured lipgloss and the person you kiss has to guess the flavour.

ABBY

(looking alarmed)
And exactly who would you both be kissing?

CHARLIE

Well, girls in the audience, obviously.

ABBY

Okaaaay?

CHARLIE gives her a kiss.

CHARLIE

Don't worry. We're winding you up!

LUCY

Guys, that's m-mean!

ABBY rolls her eyes.

ABBY

Moving on . . . If you've finished plugging your channel on our vlog, guys, I've prepared a fun idea for us to do today, since both Lucy and Charlie are here. It's the Best Friend vs Boyfriend Challenge.

JOSH

Where do I fit in?

ABBY

This doesn't involve you, Josh. You can sit there and look pretty.

JOSH rolls his eyes.

LUCY

(giggling)

Can we g-get started, guys?

ABBY

OK. So I have a list of questions on my phone that'll show how well you really know me. The first person who gives the right answer gets a point. Are you ready?

CHARLIE

Don't we need a buzzer or something?

ABBY

No, you both write your answers on these whiteboards.

ABBY hands each of them a whiteboard then consults her phone.

ABBY

First question, easy one to start . . . What's my favourite chocolate bar?

LUCY writes 'Twix'.

ABBY (CONTINUED)

Close! I do love them, but it's not my absolute fave . . .

CHARLIE writes 'Crunchie'.

ABBY (CONTINUED)

Yes!

The score comes up on the screen: 1 to Charlie, 0 to Lucy.

ABBY (CONTINUED)

One point to Charlie. Question two: What's my star sign?

CHARLIE looks blank.

LUCY writes 'Gemini'.

ABBY (CONTINUED)

Correct! One point to Lucy.

(to Charlie)

What kind of a boyfriend are you?

JOSH

Oh, nobody cares about star signs, sis!

ABBY

Josh, stay out of it. Three: Who was my first celebrity crush?

CHARLIE

No idea! I didn't know you back then.

ABBY

Well, you should still know these things about me.

LUCY

I've only known you a year, but let me think . . .

CHARLIE writes 'Harry Styles'.

ABBY

Nope . . . before that? I've definitely told both of you.

LUCY

I know!

LUCY writes 'Justin Bieber'. JOSH pulls a face.

ABBY

Yes! Lucy has two points now. Next question . . . If I was feeling down and you wanted to make me some nice comfort food, what would it be?

CHARLIE

That's a tough one.

LUCY writes furiously, then turns her board round. LUCY has written 'Mac 'n' cheese! Caesar salad! Cheesy dough balls!'

ABBY

Yummy! Yes please! Charlie?

CHARLIE

I'd go for something sweet . . .

CHARLIE turns his board round. He
has written Caramel cheesecake
and hot chocolate with
marshmallows on top.

ABBY

That sounds delicious too . . . I'll give
you both a point! Between you, you've created my perfect
meal. Next question: What's my favourite TV show?

LUCY writes '*Riverdale / Pretty Little Liars*'.
CHARLIE writes '*Stranger Things*'.

ABBY

I like 'em all, but my new obsession?

LUCY

Oh! Oh! I know!

LUCY rubs out previous answer and writes Love Island.

ABBY

Yaaas! OK last question . . . What was my

biggest fear when I was little?

CHARLIE

Josh, help me!

ABBY

No, Josh, don't tell! Come on . . . I know I've

confessed this to you guys.

LUCY writes 'Afraid of the dark'.

ABBY

Everybody's afraid of that! No, something else;
something less common!

CHARLIE writes 'Snakes/bats'.

ABBY

Weirder than that!

LUCY

(shouting)

I remember! You t-told me once.

LUCY starts writing furiously again:
'Falling down the toilet'.

ABBY

Bingo! Another point to Lucy! And
Lucy is the winner!

CHARLIE

Oh well . . . I guess I've got a lot to learn!

ABBY gives CHARLIE a hug.

ABBY

You'll do better next time! Make it up to me with that

cheesecake situation you described earlier?

(to camera)

That's all for today!

ABBY, LUCY, CHARLIE and JOSH all wave.

FADE OUT.

Views: 8,437

Subscribers: 22,013

Comments:

ShyGirl1: CHABBY goals!

girlscanvlogfan: Chesterbury? You kept that quiet!

StephSaysHi: Yes please cheesy dough balls nom nom nom!

natalie_blogs: can't wait for glitter tutorial xx

billythekid: I *live* for Stranger Things.

MagicMorgan: You'll rock Chesterbury!

(scroll down to see 17 more comments)

Chapter Two:
Jessie

Jessie sprang out of bed before the alarm went off. She'd hardly slept as today was the day of the trip, and she couldn't wait to get going. She threw on her dressing gown, tiptoed past her little brother Max and went downstairs.

'Girls can vlog . . . oh yeah . . . and girls can camp . . . !' she sang to herself as she bounded down the stairs.

Jessie's dad was in the kitchen cooking eggs. 'Morning, camper! I thought you could use a bit of proper food before you hit all that junk you're planning to scoff on the trip.' He eyed the overflowing carrier bags full of crisps, energy drinks and chocolate stacked by the door. 'Then I'll give you a lift to Lucy's.'

'Thanks, you're the best dad EV-AH!' exclaimed Jessie, and gave him a hug. While it was tough on the family that her dad had lost his job, she loved seeing more of him than before. Although, with Jessie's brothers and Gabriella – the lodger – around, it was rare to have some time alone with him.

'Excited?' Mr Dunbar asked as he dished up the eggs.

'Hashtag *YES*!' said Jessie, flinging herself on to a chair with a grin. 'Sleeping outdoors will be so much fun, and I can't wait to do some canoeing and mountain biking. We might even get a chance to try surfing one day. How cool is that?'

'Sounds brilliant, Jess. And six days with your friends – as if you don't see enough of them already,' said her father with a wry smile.

'Yeah, amazing! That's the best bit,' said Jessie, trying to hide the weird feeling bubbling up inside her. Despite her excitement about the trip, she had one nagging anxiety that she didn't share with her dad. In fact, she hadn't shared it with anyone.

She was worried about spending so much time with Abby. Things hadn't really gone back to normal since the big blow-up that had happened when Jessie had missed the fashion shoot at Springdale City Farm, and Abby had publicly shot her down in flames on the vlog. Abby had since taken the vlog down after pressure from the rest of the group, but it still hurt. Abby could be quite scathing sometimes, and the fact that she was totally obsessed with Sassy didn't help when Jessie was feeling insecure. The other day, Abby had basically implied that Sassy could have come on the trip instead of her!

'Penny for your thoughts,' said her dad, tugging her hair. 'You seem to have zoned out a bit, and you're doing that crazy leg jiggle you do when you're nervous.'

'Oh, just planning some camping pranks!' Jessie laughed, pushing the unease to the back of her mind. She took a final enthusiastic forkful of eggs. 'OK, finished! I'll get dressed in my gear, then we'd better get going!'

They waited ages at Lucy's house as Lucy's parents tried to pack everything into the campervan. Her dad had a checklist that went from tents, sleeping bags, air mattresses and camping stools to torches, first-aid kit, stuff for the barbecue, fishing tackle, camping dishes, pots and pans, containers of food, the cooler with fresh stuff, rubbish bags, paper towels . . .

'Don't forget the loo paper,' shouted Lucy's mum. 'Very important!'

'That's what I said in my festival vlog!' said Abby. 'Did you watch it, Mrs L? It went up last night.'

Mrs Lockwood smiled. 'No . . . somehow I came up with that idea on my own.'

The girls added their own backpacks and got into the van. Jessie rushed in after Lucy to make sure she wouldn't be sitting next to Abby.

'OMG!' exclaimed Lucy. 'This is a t-tight squeeze. I can hardly breathe.'

Luckily Maggie, who had been running around getting overexcited, fell asleep as soon as she was in her car seat.

'I hope nobody gets carsick,' Lucy's dad said cheerfully.

'Luckily, Pu-kota isn't with us!' joked Jessie, remembering Dakota's unfortunate explosion during the school ski trip in the winter. All the girls giggled, including Abby, which made Jessie feel better about being stuck in the van with her.

'Well, it's a long drive,' said Lucy's mum, 'so I suggest you just sit back, listen to some music and chill.'

'And eat,' added Jessie, passing around a tube of salt-and-vinegar Pringles. She prided herself on always having snacks available in any given scenario.

Abby sat forward as they backed out of the driveway. 'Mrs Lockwood, is it true you used to go to Coachella and Burning Man in America? That must have been sooo cool! I mean . . . all those great bands and celebrities!' She beamed. 'Oh, and Lucy said you might still have some outfits from then. Did you bring them along?'

Mrs Lockwood laughed. 'I did pack a few for fun, but

I'm not sure the short shorts and cowboy boots are really suitable for this occasion or weather! We'll see!'

She continued, 'More seriously, though, girls, we do need to agree to some ground rules for this trip. Because we're responsible for you, we need to be sure that we always know where you are. You mustn't wander off the campsite, and we'd like you to stay in pairs or a group if you go down to the lake or the woods.'

The woods . . . Jessie zoned out as she pictured herself building a campfire, maybe making a life raft from scratch, opening up the Swiss army knife she'd been dying to use . . . Hey, maybe she could learn how to skin a rabbit, like Katniss in *The Hunger Games*!

'Just be sensible,' added Mr Lockwood, turning round and raising an eyebrow.

'We will, promise!' said Lucy.

'Promise,' echoed a newly awake Maggie solemnly.

Jessie giggled.

The girls' phones all pinged. Jessie looked at hers. It was a group message from Sassy:

09:02

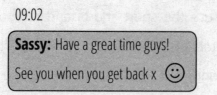

Sassy: Have a great time guys!
See you when you get back x 😊

'Aw. That's really nice of her,' said Hermione, unwrapping one of the lemon-drizzle cupcakes she'd brought with her.

'Too bad she isn't with us,' said Abby with a sigh.

Jessie stiffened, her *Hunger Games* fantasy evaporating fast.

'We'll have to FaceTime her LOADS,' continued Abby, typing out a reply.

09:02

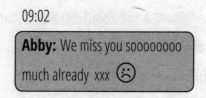

Abby: We miss you soooooooo
much already xxx 😞

Jessie couldn't help but feel upset as she glanced at Abby's message on the screen. A few weeks ago, they hadn't even met Sassy, and now the whole trip was ruined because she wasn't here?

'Actually, I was thinking perhaps you girls might want to have less screen time while you're away,' said Lucy's mum. 'Get back to nature, enjoy the peace and quiet. I know you'll want to vlog, but you can cut down on other stuff . . . A digital detox, isn't that what they call it?'

'My mum said the same thing,' said Hermione. 'Apart from when I need to call home.'

Abby pouted. 'Well, maybe we could FaceTime just once or twice, then. If we get a signal. It won't be the same without her otherwise . . .' She trailed off sadly.

'Jeez, Abs! We get the message!' snapped Jessie.

Lucy's mum glanced round in surprise at her sharp tone. Jessie knew she was being dramatic, but, honestly, she was so fed up of this Sassy worship! She was pretty sure that half the time Abby was doing it to get to her – and it was working.

'I was only saying . . .' muttered Abby.

'So, who's for carpool karaoke?' asked Lucy's dad brightly after an awkward pause.

Jessie was still too hurt to speak and glared down at her phone.

'Me! What's the f-first song?' said Lucy, and gave Jessie's hand a squeeze, while Hermione chucked a cupcake in Jessie's direction.

'Wow, this is amazing,' exclaimed Jessie five hours later as they pulled into their camping spot at Blackwater Lake Campsite. Her mood had improved massively – she was on a sugar high from cupcakes and pick-and-mix, and had successfully avoided any more run-ins with Abby. She looked out of the window at the hundreds of trees surrounding the campsite and the big, calm lake in the distance. 'This place is enormous!'

'Can we g-go exploring?' asked Lucy.

'First we need help unloading the van and setting up the tents,' said Mr Lockwood. 'After that, explore to your hearts' content.'

They piled out of the van, and Jessie was soon helping Mr Lockwood lay down the ground sheets, drive in the pegs and put up the tents. There were two: a four-person one for Lucy's parents and Maggie, and a six-person tent for the girls.

'I can see you've done this before, Jessie,' said Lucy's dad. 'Thank heavens there's at least one practical person among you!'

'Daa-ad!' protested Lucy.

Jessie smiled gratefully. 'Well, I've been camping before and, anyway, I build lots of construction kits, like LEGO and stuff, with my brothers, so I'm used to following instructions.'

'You should consider engineering as a career. You'd be good at it,' said Mr Lockwood.

'Hmm, never really thought about it,' said Jessie, pleased by the compliment.

Mr Lockwood handed her the final peg, and she used her boot to work it into the ground. The girls stuck their heads into the tent.

Snug but cosy, Jessie thought happily. They spread their sleeping bags and pillows on the air mattresses and stowed their bags.

'I brought some fairy lights and candles to decorate the tent,' said Abby, pulling them out of her bag.

'Fairy l-lights? You idiot! Where did you think you'd p-plug them in? There's no electricity!' said Lucy, giggling.

'No candles allowed either, I'm afraid,' said Lucy's mum. 'Fire hazard!'

Abby sighed. 'Oh, I hadn't thought of that . . . Such a shame, as this one smells amazing, sort of like a campfire.'

We'll have an actual campfire, thought Jessie, suddenly irritated again. *Why is nothing ever good enough for her?* She told herself to calm down.

'Mrs Lockwood, is there anywhere for me to hang my mosquito net?' asked Hermione hesitantly. 'I've also packed quite a few types of insect repellant, but my mum thought I should use a net for extra protection.'

Jessie sighed. She couldn't believe what a fuss everyone was making – she didn't care about lighting or insects. Why couldn't they hurry up and get exploring?

'I'm sure we'll find a way of hanging it,' Lucy's mum told Hermione. 'Of course, we can't guarantee you won't get bitten: this is the great outdoors after all!' She glanced at Jessie who was chomping at the bit. 'OK, girls, off you go . . . but be back by five so we can prepare our first campfire supper.'

'Will do! See ya, Mrs L!' said Jessie cheerfully. 'Right, gang, where shall we go first? The lake?'

'Let's check out the loos first,' said Abby. 'I'm desperate!'

Jessie groaned.

'I'll g-go with her,' said Lucy quickly. 'We'll m-meet you two down by the l-lake.'

Jessie smiled gratefully at Lucy as she and Abby hurried off, following the sign to the shower block.

Jessie skipped happily down the path through the woods, then glanced back at Hermione, lingering behind her. She slowed down.

'You're being kind of quiet, H,' she said, noticing Hermione's worried expression. 'Are you OK? Still stressed about the insects? They won't kill you, promise!'

Hermione shook her head. 'It's not just that. More . . . stuff at home. It's been on my mind for a while. My dad still wants me to meet his new girlfriend's daughter when we get back . . . That's so not happening while I have a say!'

Jessie smiled sympathetically. She knew she would hate it if her parents separated and she was expected to get on brilliantly with a whole new family.

'Plus, yeah, I am a bit anxious about this camping stuff to be honest,' continued Hermione. 'Not just the mosquitos – but everything! How am I going to be able to read at night?'

Jessie laughed. Reading was the last thing on her mind! 'You're so cute . . . You'll just have to detox from reading, I guess.' She paused, then glanced back at Hermione. 'Actually, I've got something bothering me too. Can I tell you? You can't tell the others . . .'

'Promise. Go on, spill,' said Hermione curiously.

'Well, it's about me and Abby . . .' said Jessie. She paused, trying to find the right words. 'I mean, I can tell she still hates me for that fashion-shoot disaster. Everyone thinks we made up when I helped her with her panic attack at SummerTube, but that hasn't really lasted. I know I let you guys down, but it wasn't deliberate, and I felt awful about it. And now Abby is still mean to me and it really hurts. Especially when she goes on about how amazing Sassy is.'

Jessie exhaled loudly. It felt good to have finally told someone how she felt.

'Oh, Jess!' said Hermione, reaching over to give her a hug. 'She has been giving you a bit of a hard time. I guess I didn't really pay attention because I wanted us all to be OK again. Abby can sometimes be kind of . . .'

'Nasty?' interjected Jessie bitterly.

'I was going to say harsh,' said Hermione. 'Sometimes she doesn't think before she speaks. And she can be quite spiky. Like in the car today with the Sassy stuff – we all noticed that. I honestly don't think she means to hurt anyone, though.'

Jessie felt irritated. Did Hermione actually believe that? 'Well, it doesn't feel like that from where I'm standing,' she replied. 'It's got to the point where I'm not completely comfortable around her any more. And she's sooo precious sometimes.' Jessie hated complaining, but now that she'd started, it was hard to stop. These feelings had been building up for ages, and it was such a relief to let them out.

'Hmm,' said Hermione, looking anxious. 'Leave it with me, Jess. Let me think about it.' Her voice perked up. 'And look! How gorgeous is that!'

Jessie followed her gaze. They had reached the dock on the lake where there were kayaks for rent outside a little boathouse, waterskiing equipment and a cafe. The lake itself was large and beautiful with a little island in the middle. Hermione got out her phone and started taking pictures.

'Seriously nice,' agreed Jessie. She took in the inflatable water park, which featured slippery walkways, slides and swings and, to her delight, water trampolines. They'd be able to film some amazing footage here.

'Wait up, you guys!'

Jessie stiffened as she heard Abby's call. She and Lucy were running to catch up with them.

'OMG, guys!' Abby continued, breathless. 'We've just struck it lucky. Guess what we spotted?'

'Some kind of wildlife?' said Hermione nervously.

Abby snorted. 'Wildlife? I guess you could call it that. We saw these really rare specimens. They were too far away to talk to and, anyway, we don't want to seem keen—'

'You mean boys?' asked Hermione.

'Yes – cute ones! Our age, I think. We can get the binoculars out and stalk them!' said Abby.

'Obviously I'm taken!' Lucy smiled, 'But they were OK-looking I g-guess!'

'We don't know them,' said Hermione. 'I'm not following some randoms around all day.'

Jessie agreed – she knew what Abby was like; they

might lose a whole day to boy watching. 'Also, errr, Lucy's not the only taken one, remember, Abby?' she added. Charlie was friends with all of them, and he was crazy about Abby since they'd officially got together a few weeks ago. 'He was so cute with you in that Best Friend/BF challenge.'

'So?' said Abby sharply. 'It's early days with me and Charlie . . . Besides, am I not allowed to talk to other guys?'

Jessie cleared her throat. Abby had suddenly made her feel like a baby. 'Of course you are – you said you wanted to stalk them, though,' she said defensively. 'Sounds a bit weird if you're not interested, that's all. But whatever. Forget I said anything.'

'I will,' said Abby breezily. She looked down at her phone. 'Sassy says she would have been up for boy-spotting . . . oh well.'

Jessie huffed and was relieved when Hermione and Lucy started talking loudly about their vlog ideas for the week.

It was ages until supper was ready. The fire took a long time to get hot enough to cook their hotdogs.

They had corn on the cob and baked beans as well.

'Dee-licious,' said Jessie. 'Why does food always taste better outdoors?'

'Mom, can we have the marshmallows nowww?' begged Maggie for the fifth time.

Jessie smiled at her – toasting marshmallows had been her favourite part of camping at Maggie's age too. And it was still up there, if she was honest.

'Sure, Mags, I'll help you,' said Lucy, scooting over to sit next to her sister. 'Put your m-marshmallow on the end of the roasting stick. Careful of the pointy tip! Now hold it over the campfire, but careful not to let it catch f-fire!'

'Yum yum yum!' mumbled Maggie, her mouth full of marshmallow, a few minutes later.

'Watch out! Y-you've got it all in your hair!' cried Lucy.

Jessie leaned over and dabbed at Maggie's hair. 'Don't worry, Mags. Max would have made an even bigger mess! There we go – that's clean enough.'

'Thanks, Jessie. OK, princess,' said Mrs Lockwood. 'Time for bed. Say goodnight to the girls. You'll see them in the morning.'

'This is so relaxing,' said Hermione as they sat round the campfire on their own after doing the washing-up. They were sipping cocoa and eating more marshmallows, and Abby had her vlog camera out.

'You OK?' Hermione mouthed to Jessie, who nodded. Jessie had sort of been avoiding Abby after what had happened down by the lake, not wanting to make a big deal of it.

Lucy gestured at Abby to film her. 'Here, guys, is h-how you make smores,' she said as she took a toasted marshmallow and a melted chunk of chocolate and sandwiched them between two digestive biscuits. 'This is a MUST on every c-camping trip in America.' She took a huge bite.

'This is so good,' said Hermione, shoving one in her mouth and licking her fingers.

'What shall we do now?' asked Jessie, once they'd all had one. 'Tell ghost stories or play truth or dare?'

VLOG 2

Festival Dos and Don'ts

`4:57`

FADE IN: ABBY'S BEDROOM

ABBY sitting on her bed with WEENIE on her lap, wearing pink-and-red tartan pyjamas. Bed is covered with clothes and toiletries and a half-empty camping rucksack.

ABBY

Hi, guys! Sorry for the mess – it's shocking, I know – but I'm in the middle of packing. I'm going camping with the Girls Can

Vlog crew, which OBVIOUSLY we'll be vlogging, but the really exciting part – as some of you picked up in our last vlog – is that we're also going to Chesterbury! Yay! And so today I'm going to give you ten tips on how to make your festival visit a big success and some pitfalls to avoid. So here goes . . . Oops, bye, Weenie!

WEENIE jumps off her lap.

ABBY (CONTINUED)

First up, be organized and plan in advance. Make lists of what you're going to pack.

ABBY holds up a clipboard.

ABBY (CONTINUED)

When you leave home, make sure you've got your ticket, money and phone. Oh, and to help you coordinate with your mates, set up a WhatsApp group for everyone who's going – great for sharing plans both before the festival and when you're there. Agree a meeting place in case you get separated.

Still on planning . . . work out your outfits for each day ahead of time. Don't just pack lots of random clothes, cos you're bound to pack too much and leave behind the most important thingS. Go through it day by day: clothes, shoes, accessories. This is a tough one for me as I always want to bring my entire floordrobe!

MONTAGE: ABBY trying to fit too many clothes into a heaving suitcase, tries to zip it up but can't.

ABBY (CONTINUED)

Phone. Obviously don't forget it, as it's crucial to stay in touch with your friends. VERY IMPORTANT – pack a spare battery. And, while you're there, turn off your data to save battery. If it's going to rain, keep your phone safe in a Ziploc bag.

Which leads me to the next point. Prepare for all weather. Bring sunscreen, a hat and sunglasses, but only cheapies in case you lose or break them. Choose some fun ones that'll look great on Instagram.

ABBY models some fluorescent-pink star-shaped sunglasses.

ABBY (CONTINUED)
If you're going somewhere it might rain, take a waterproof jacket and some wellies. Wear something you feel comfortable in, especially on your feet. No heels, sandals or open-toed shoes. Sad, I know – I'm gonna have to leave these little beauties behind!

ABBY holds up a pair of strappy sandals.

ABBY (CONTINUED)
Your feet will get trampled and filthy. Boots can give you

blisters, so basically trainers are your best bet. Take a mini dry shampoo. You can get them in so many gorgeous scents now. My favourite is rose. Don't pack anything valuable like jewellery. Stay hydrated. Take a refillable water bottle so you don't have to keep buying plastic ones – saves money and the environment! Loo roll. Loo roll, loo roll, loo roll.

ABBY laughs.

ABBY (CONTINUED)
Most important, bring your FUN self. Stay safe and have a fantastic time! So I hope that's helped you guys get ready for a festival! Now I've gotta get back to my packing! I just can't decide about tops. If you've got any other great tips, put them in the comments down below, and I'll give you a shout-out next week. And look out for my next 'Get Ready with Me' festival vlog. Bye-ee!

ABBY waves to the camera.

FADE OUT.

Views: 10,289

Subscribers: 23,766

Comments:

girlscanvlogfan: #earlysquad

ShyGirl1: wish i was coming too.

xxrainbowxx: please tag your pjs!!

cactuscollector: Love you, Abby xxx

festivalchick100: you forgot wet wipes – portable shower in a packet!

(scroll down to see 24 more comments)

Chapter Three: Abby

There was a loud whispering noise, and Abby woke with a jolt. Where was she? All she could see was blue surrounding her. She looked through the darkness and saw a body stretched out beside her . . . OF COURSE! She was in a tent with her mates – they were camping.

The body sat up and whispered, 'Abs, did you hear that?'

'What, Hermione?' croaked Abby, still half asleep.

'That! That rustling sound. I keep hearing it.'

'Hmmm.' Abby tried to listen hard. 'Maybe?' she replied. It was probably Hermione's overactive imagination playing tricks again.

Hermione grabbed her hand. 'There it is again! What is it? It could be, like, a giant cockroach or something.' Her voice was growing shrill.

Abby grinned in the dark. 'It's OK, H, don't panic.' Although . . . Abby could definitely hear some scratching in the tent now too.

'OMG!' Hermione screamed. 'Something just ran across my face! HELP!'

She tried to jump up, still in her sleeping bag, and tripped over Lucy, who was next to her. Abby giggled. She'd never seen Hermione move so fast before.

'Keep your hair on, dude,' she said as Hermione continued to scream from where she'd fallen. 'It's probably nothing.'

Hermione ignored her and kept wailing.

'Or, you know, just keep screaming . . .' Abby was half tempted to grab the vlog camera – this was hilarious.

'What's g-going on?' asked Lucy, sitting up. 'Get the t-torch!'

'It's probably nothing,' said Abby again, glancing at Hermione, who had now hidden her face in her hands. 'Just H's creepy-crawly phobia kicking into action.'

Suddenly there was light; Jessie had switched on the

torch and was shining it around. 'What do you think you saw, H?'

'I didn't see it – I felt it!' Hermione shuddered. 'I don't know what it was, but it's freaking me right out . . .'

Jessie pointed the torch at the corner of the tent where they'd stashed their snacks. Abby shrieked as she caught sight of a brown creature desperately scrabbling to get out of a large packet of M&Ms.

'It's a rat!' she shouted, feeling a rush of panic. 'Oooh, get it out of here! Lucy! Look – it's already nibbled the chocolate! Gross!'

'Keep your hair on, dude,' she heard Jessie mumble.

Abby shot her a look in the gloom. 'What is that supposed to mean?' It seemed like Jessie was always trying to pick a fight with her at the moment. She edged away from the rat.

'Just – you weren't the most sympathetic to Hermione just now,' said Jessie with a shrug.

Abby rolled her eyes. This was ridiculous. 'I was obviously joking! Plus, I think Hermione can speak for herself, thanks, Jessie. H – do you have a problem with me?'

'Guys, this is not the time,' pleaded Hermione. 'Can we concentrate on getting the rat out, ASAP?!'

'It looks m-more like a mouse,' said Lucy. 'Kind of cute, actually. It's t-tiny and so frightened cos it can't get out.'

'I'll call the RSPCA, shall I?' said Abby sarcastically, feeling increasingly disgusted. Didn't rats or mice or whatever carry diseases? 'Just get it out, someone.'

'I'm on it, Abs.' Lucy got up, unzipped the tent, and eventually the mouse ran out into the night.

'That bag of chocolate must have seemed like a treasure trove to that littleun,' said Jessie. 'You can see where it was nibbling through the packet . . . We should have known better than to keep food in the tent.'

'We're lucky we weren't in America where it m-might have been a b-bear.' Lucy laughed.

'Don't!' said Hermione. 'I'm probably going to have nightmares now as it is.'

Eventually they all got back to sleep, Abby tossing and turning for a while as she replayed Jessie's comments in her mind. She knew she wasn't always the most touchy-feely of people, but on the whole she was a nice person, wasn't she? If not, why were they all friends with her?

Now it was morning. Abby yawned, reached under her pillow for her phone and started catching up on Snapchat and Instagram. She already felt a million miles away from all the stuff going on back home and looked longingly at a beauty blogger's flat lay of a new range of perfumes. She Snapchatted with Sassy (who said she was dying of boredom) for a while, then—

'Rise and shine, guys,' chirped Lucy, sitting up and stretching. 'I p-promised my mom we'd help cook b-breakfast. There's pancake mix, so it sh-should be easy.'

'On it!' said Hermione eagerly.

Abby was relieved someone else had offered – she wasn't a fan of cooking first thing in the morning.

As it was a bit cramped with all of them in one tent, they took turns getting ready. Hermione and Jessie went first, then went to help with breakfast. Abby and Lucy headed off to the shower block, Abby holding her wash bag, which was crammed with mini toiletries.

'Luce, can you plait my hair?' she asked. 'It'll help keep it clean for a few days. Plus those French plaits look kinda cute?' She wanted to look nice for later if they saw those boys again . . . even though she had zero plans to do anything, despite what Jessie thought.

Lucy nodded. 'Sure thing. And, Abs, I have something I n-need to talk to you about.'

Abby sensed a seriousness in Lucy's voice. *What now?*

'It's a b-bit tricky,' said Lucy. 'I r-really don't want to h-hurt your f-feelings . . .'

Abby noticed that Lucy's stammer was worse than usual because she was nervous. Was it something really bad?

'It's about you and J-Jess,' Lucy continued.

Abby's heart sank. She knew things were awkward, but hadn't realized the others were aware of it too.

'Jess? What's the problem?' She tried to sound breezy.

'Well, Abs, ever since the f-fashion shoot at C-City Farm and all that, there's b-been a problem. I m-mean you never really m-made it up with Jessie. She told Hermione that she th-thinks you still hate her. Oh, this is r-really hard for me, Abs.' She took Abby's hand. 'That photoshoot video was quite v-vicious, and sometimes you can be very s-snarky to Jess. We've all n-noticed it.'

Abby pulled back her hand, feeling suddenly sick, as if she'd been punched. She didn't know what to say.

'This is ridiculous! Complete rubbish!' she hit back as they reached the shower block. 'I mean, the fashion shoot was Jessie's fault, and I can't believe she's still whining about it.'

In a tense silence, they brushed their teeth, washed their faces, then brushed their hair. Abby massaged on some moisturiser with inbuilt SPF and a slight tint. A million angry thoughts were going through her

mind, but she didn't want to say the wrong
thing and fall out with Lucy too.

'Shall I p-plait your hair, then?' asked Lucy after
a while.

Abby nodded, relieved at the change of subject. She
sat on a little stool, with Lucy standing behind her, and
stared into the mirror.

Finally she asked, 'Is it really that bad – I mean with
Jess? I noticed she was snappy with me in the night.'

Lucy nodded. "Fraid so. Did you ever a-apologize for
shaming her on the v-vlog?'

'Of course!' replied Abby instantly. But, when she
thought about it, she wasn't sure that she really had . . .

They got back to the campsite where the pancakes
were ready, and crispy bacon too. It smelt absolutely
delicious.

'I'm starved!' said Jessie, passing round some maple
syrup. 'Shall we see who can eat the most pancakes in a
minute? It'd make a good vlog!'

'I can, I can!' shouted Maggie, running around with great excitement.

Lucy's dad agreed to film them, and Jessie started setting up the camera.

She seems fine, thought Abby, watching Jessie wrangle with the tripod. *Honestly, what is all the fuss about?*

It was a warm day, so after breakfast they headed down to the lake in their swimwear. Lucy's parents had arranged for them to rent some kayaks.

Abby and Hermione sunbathed on the dock while Jessie and Lucy sorted out the kayaks and life jackets. They'd decided to pair up and get two-person kayaks.

'Check out my new bikini,' said Abby, doing a little twirl. 'I got it at Topshop.' It was turquoise with tiny silver hearts printed on it, and she was so excited to get the chance to finally wear it.

'Love the colour,' said Hermione. 'And your shades are cool! Can I borrow some of your sunscreen?'

Abby passed it over. 'Shall we share a boat, H?' she asked. She wanted to avoid Jessie and Lucy if possible. She wasn't ready yet to think about what Lucy had said.

'Of course, ' said Hermione, 'but I'll probably be useless as I've never been in a kayak before. '

'Me neither, but I'm sure it's a piece of cake,' replied Abby, scanning the lake. 'So where do you think those boys are today? Maybe we'll see them when we get out on the lake. There are some other kayaks out there already.'

'Perfect,' muttered Hermione. 'Now I get to capsize in front of a load of random guys.'

Abby laughed. 'You'll be fine, H, trust me!'

Once the girls had their life jackets on, Lucy and Jessie climbed into the first kayak. Abby watched as they paddled around in a circle and came back to the dock.

'This is brilliant!' exclaimed Jessie. 'OK, guys. Your turn!'

Abby noticed that despite her friendly tone, she only looked at Hermione as she spoke.

'Abby, you go up to the front. I'll get in the back,' said Hermione nervously, eyeing the second canoe.

'No problem!' said Abby, used to being the brave one. She stepped into the kayak – it was wobblier than she'd expected – then SPLASH! Before she knew it, Abby had fallen into the freezing cold lake.

'HELP!' she cried, treading water and looking around for sharks . . . or, wait, maybe didn't they live in lakes? There was the Loch Ness monster, but she was pretty sure that was in Scotland. Still yelping, she started swimming towards the dock.

'Abs!' the others shrieked. 'Are you OK?' Even Jessie looked concerned.

'GIRL OVERBOARD!' Abby heard someone shout, followed by lots of laughter.

Two kayaks came into view – with four boys paddling towards them. It looked like the guys she had spotted yesterday. Hermione's nightmare had happened to her!

'Made a bit of a splash, didn't you?' one of them said with a cheeky grin.

'Not funny,' she choked through a mouthful of water.

Hermione helped Abby out of the lake and back on to the dock. Abby gave herself a bit of a shake and thought it was lucky that her hair was in plaits. *At least I don't have straggly wet rat tails*. She straightened out her baseball cap and wrapped a towel around herself.

'Just testing the water to see if it was wet!' she called to the boys.

'L-let's try again,' said Lucy as they all regrouped on the dock. 'Maybe Hermione should g-go with you, Jess, and I'll p-pair up with Abby so we have somebody with experience in each b-boat.'

Soon both kayaks were back on the lake and the girls were paddling out.

'This is fun!' exclaimed Abby, looking around to see where the boys had got to. 'Oh, here they come,' she whispered to Lucy as one of the kayaks surged through the water in their direction.

'Hey, fancy a race round the island and back?' called out the dark-haired boy in the stern.

'I'm game,' replied Abby and looked over to Jessie, who was nodding.

'Yeah. Let's do this!' said Jessie.

Abby grinned. When it came to boys versus girls, they could forget their stupid fight and join together in solidarity.

The kayak race was a bit of a shambles as the boys were clearly more experienced than the girls. It was harder than it looked to stay on course and go fast, and Abby and Lucy capsized again. It was really fun, though, and when they'd finally all come back to the dock, they got ice creams and hung out together, laughing and chatting.

'What are you guys doing tonight?' Abby asked Finn, the dark-haired one. She ignored Jessie, who was raising her eyebrow behind Finn.

She honestly thinks I'm not allowed to speak to boys who aren't Charlie, thought Abby. *So annoying* . . . Plus, the only reason she was suggesting hanging out was that she'd noticed Hermione glancing repeatedly at Leo,

Finn's friend with the white-blond hair and a
bad case of sunburn. He seemed just as shy
as Hermione, so, if her hunch was correct, the bashful
pair would need some help. If there was one thing Abby
loved, it was a good match-making opportunity.

Finn shrugged. 'Dunno, nothing special.'

'No, nothing,' Leo added, reddening slightly.

'Neither are we,' said Hermione earnestly. 'Well, you
know, we're cooking some food, obviously, but not much
else, well, washing out our pans ha ha . . . ' She trailed off
awkwardly and looked to Abby for help.

Abby smiled and dived in to rescue her. 'Yeah, so
anyway, guys, maybe you could come over to our
campsite and hang out after dinner? We could play
some games?' She quickly looked at Lucy to check that
it was OK.

Lucy shrugged. 'I'll ask my p-parents, but I'm sure it's
fine.'

'Cool, we're in!' said Finn after consulting with his
friends. 'Laters.'

Abby smiled and mentally started planning outfits for Hermione. At least with the boys there, she wouldn't be stuck dealing with Jessie's issues and Lucy trying to guilt-trip her!

VLOG 3

What's In My Mouth?

9:33

FADE IN: ABBY, LUCY, JESSIE , HERMIONE, LEO and FINN sitting around the campfire.

JESSIE

Hey, guys! So here we are at the campsite with some new friends, Leo and Finn. Hoping we can upload this at the cafe here, which sometimes has Wi-Fi . . . fingers crossed.
Say hi, guys.

LEO and FINN wave.

JESSIE (CONTINUED)

Today we thought we'd do some fun challenges. We're kicking

off with the 'What's in My Mouth' challenge, where people are

blindfolded and have to guess the thing that's placed in their

mouth. It could be edible or not! So we've got a girls team with

Lucy and Hermione, and a boys team with Leo and Finn.

Abby, please put on the blindfolds!

ABBY ties bandanas round the eyes of the four contestants.

ABBY

Are you ready?

LUCY

Yes! As w-we'll ever be.

JESSIE

OK, here we go.

ABBY approaches FINN, holding a spoon.

ABBY

Open wide, Finn. No – wider!

FINN

I don't like this.

(laughs)

And I don't trust you.

ABBY

You don't trust me? Oh well, that's a shame. Open up!

FINN opens his mouth slowly, and ABBY pops in the spoon.

ABBY (CONTINUED)

Go on, swallow it! It's safe.

ABBY laughs. FINN swallows, and a few seconds later, leaps up, yelping.

FINN

Aargh! It's really hot! It's burning my mouth!

Get me a glass of water!

ABBY

(giggling)

Here you go.

ABBY hands him a glass of water.

ABBY (CONTINUED)

Can you guess what it is?

FINN

(fanning his mouth)

Chili sauce? Tabasco? OMG. It

feels like my lips are on fire . . .

JESSIE

Boom, you nailed it! Tabasco.

One point for the boys' team. Next up is LEO.

LEO

This is unsettling . . . the fear of the unknown and all that.

HERMIONE

(fiddling with her blindfold)

I know the feeling.

ABBY

Open wide, Leo!

ABBY puts the tip of a make-up brush into LEO's mouth. LEO spits out the brush.

LEO

Ugh! It's furry. Sort of
tickly. Like a bumblebee.

ABBY

As if I'd put a bee in your mouth! Guess again.

LEO

A soft toy? I don't know. I give up . . .

ABBY

(exclaims)

It's a make-up brush!

LEO rips off his bandana to look at it.

LEO

What! No way.

JESSIE

No points for you, soz. OK, girls, now it's your turn . . .

Hermione, open up! I've got a spoonful of something for you.

HERMIONE

Oh God, I hope it's not Tabasco again.

JESSIE puts the spoon into HERMIONE's mouth. HERMIONE swallows slowly and pulls a face.

HERMIONE

Oof! It's really sour. Lemon juice?

JESSIE

Not quite.

HERMIONE

Lime! Lime juice!

JESSIE

Yessss! One point for the girls team. Next up, Lucy.

LUCY

Be kind!

JESSIE

Stick out your tongue.

JESSIE places a cotton-wool ball on LUCY's tongue.

LUCY

Eeew! W-what is it?

LUCY raises her hands to remove it.

JESSIE

Hands down! You're not allowed to touch. You can only use your mouth.

LUCY tries to spit out the ball and fails.

LUCY

It's stuck to my t-tongue! Is it a t-tissue maybe?

JESSIE

Close, but not quite. Guess again!

LUCY

Dunno. I g-give up. It's gross.

JESSIE

Cotton-wool ball! So, guys, it's a draw . . . one all.

Last round to decide the winner.

ABBY

OK, Finn. Open up. I'm gonna put the whole thing in your

mouth.

ABBY places a prawn on to
FINN's tongue.

FINN

Argh! It smells fishy, but it
feels like a worm.

(shouting)

IS IT A WORM? I'll kill you.

ABBY

(laughing hysterically)

No, it's not a worm. It's food. You can give it a little chew . . .

FINN

I'm not doing that!

FINN spits it into his hand.

FINN

I give up.

JESSIE

It's just a prawn!

FINN

I was close. It did smell like fish.

JESSIE

Soz. OK, Leo, you're up next. Bandana back on, please!

LEO pulls the bandana back over his eyes

LEO

Ready.

ABBY places an olive into his mouth.

LEO (CONTINUED)

Ooh . . . it's round and smooth. It might be a grape, but it tastes a bit salty. Maybe a pickled onion. Is it safe to chew?

JESSIE

Sure.

LEO bites into the olive.

LEO

Oh – olive!

JESSIE

Bingo! Two points for the boys. Now, Hermione, here comes

another spoonful.

HERMIONE

I'll try to be brave.

ABBY places a spoon into HERMIONE's mouth.

HERMIONE (CONTINUED)

Yuck, it's slimy and sharp. Quite hot.

(thinks)

I thought it was mayo, but now I'm thinking mustard.

JESSIE

Woohoo! Another point for the girls . . . so it's two–two.

Now, Lucy, it's all down to you.

HERMIONE

(laughing)

No pressure, Luce!

LUCY

Bring it on!

ABBY places a piece of raw broccoli in LUCY's mouth.

LUCY (CONTINUED)

Eew! It smells kind of like

B-Brussels sprouts . . .

JESSIE

Go on, give it a chew.

LUCY crunches the broccoli.

JESSIE (CONTINUED)

Whadaya think?

LUCY pulls a face.

LUCY

B-broccoli. Raw.

ABBY

(shouting)

Hooray! You're right. Girls win! Three–two.

Everyone removes their bandanas.

HERMIONE

I've got a consolation prize for you, Leo. Some homemade

cookies from back home.

HERMIONE opens up a tin and passes it to LEO.

LEO

Amazing, thanks!

FINN

Er, what about me?

HERMIONE looks suddenly
embarrassed.

HERMIONE

Oh yeah, sorry, for you too. That's what I meant.

HERMIONE passes FINN the tin, and he shakes his head in
mock outrage.

JESSIE

(to camera)

So, I hope you all enjoyed this video, guys. Give us a thumbs-
up down below and watch out for our next video from
Blackwater Lake. Bye!

They all wave.

FADE OUT as they continue chatting and eating.

Views: 14,701

Subscribers: 24,213

Comments:

StephSaysHi: If someone put a prawn in my mouth, I would freak. Out.

evie_bakes: Anyone else think Hermione has a thing for Leo?

(Reply: **pink_sparkles:** Totally! 🖤)

miavlogs: Tabasco is amazing. I put it in everything xx

foodchallengeking: These were soo easy!

(scroll down to see 35 more comments)

Chapter Four: Hermione

Hermione woke feeling ravenous, despite all the cookies she'd eaten the night before, after a better night's sleep. The mouse hadn't made a reappearance, and even the mosquitoes had left her in peace. Things were looking up!

She'd actually enjoyed the evening round the campfire with the boys from the campsite. Leo had turned out to be a big Harry Potter fan, and they'd had quite a bit to talk about, even though he (gasp) hadn't read the books, only seen the films. Usually Hermione would be annoyed by this, but for some reason she could forgive Leo . . . Plus his sunburn was weirdly kind of cute.

'Knock, knock . . .' said Lucy's dad, outside the tent. 'Everybody decent?'

'Yeah,' said Hermione, looking around. The others

were still snoozing. 'Decent and mostly asleep!'

'Well, consider this your hotel wake-up call,' said Mr Lockwood, poking his head in. 'We have a new guest joining us later today, and we need to prepare—'

'Sassy, Sassy, Sassy,' cried Maggie, running in past her dad. 'Sassy's coming!' She launched herself on to Lucy's sleeping bag.

'Huh?' said Hermione, confused.

At the same time, Abby sat up. 'OMG, really? She said yesterday she was trying to get her dad to drive her, but I didn't think he actually would! AMAZING!' She reached for her phone and started tapping excitedly at the screen.

Hermione looked anxiously at Jessie, who had also woken up in all the commotion.

'Sassy's coming?' Surprise flickered over Jessie's face, 'Cool,' she said simply.

Hermione gave her a little smile. She could tell Jessie was trying to be mature about the whole thing.

'Thanks f-for organizing that, Dad,' said Lucy.

'When are they coming?'

'Couple of hours, maybe – they made an early start,' said Mr Lockwood. 'Sassy's father says she was miserable on her own, knowing you were all here, poor girl! He's sorted a Chesterbury ticket too. I'll need to drive you girls over early and then come back for your mother and Maggie when we go, as we won't all fit otherwise. And I'm hoping we can squeeze Sassy into your tent.'

'Yeah, totally, Mr L. She can sleep here next to me,' said Abby, looking up from her phone and patting the tiny spot next to her. 'Acres of room.'

'So cool, and now that the f-five of us can do some vlogs together, our viewers will be so h-happy. Off you g-get, monkey,' Lucy said to Maggie. 'Dad, do you still w-want me to babysit this morning?'

'Yes, we're going food shopping. We're running dangerously low on supplies – especially now that we'll have another mouth to feed.' He waved at Maggie. 'She's all yours – see ya, kiddo! . . . OK, I'm out of here.' Mr Lockwood spluttered as Abby spritzed herself with a cloud of floral deodorant, and crawled back out of the tent.

Hermione waved her hands about in the air. 'Abs, I think you're good now. You probably don't need to reapply for at least a year,' she said, laughing at the sour look she got in response.

'So, Mags, I thought we'd g-go to the adventure playground,' said Lucy. 'Would you like that?'

Maggie nodded eagerly.

'Anyone w-wanna join us?'

'I'll come with you, Luce,' Hermione offered. She'd been waiting for an opportunity to catch up with Lucy alone – maybe this was her chance.

'I might sunbathe at the lake,' said Abby, and, 'Lake for me,' said Jessie at the same time.

There was a pause, then: 'Yeah, I'm dying to get back in that kayak,' said Jessie. 'We can walk down together, if it's OK with you, Abby?'

Hermione held her breath. This was so awkward – when had they ever had to ask each other permission to do things? She glanced at Lucy, who was also looking nervous.

'Of course it's OK!' said Abby sharply. 'Come on, let's get ready. We want to be back in time to welcome Sassy.'

'Of course we do,' mumbled Jessie, tugging at her pyjama top.

As they walked over to the playground, Lucy asked Hermione, 'So, H, are you having a g-good time? I know you were a bit n-nervous about the camping stuff, but last night was fun . . .'

Hermione nodded. 'Totally.' She wondered if Lucy wanted her to say something about Leo, but if so, she didn't feel like discussing it yet. She didn't even know what 'it' was. 'Don't worry about me,' she continued. 'I'm loving it . . . but we MAY have a problem with Abby and Jessie. I told you about Jessie being upset by Abby, and I think with Sassy coming we might be in for a major explosion!'

'I know,' agreed Lucy. 'But I don't think Abby r-realizes

she's being mean, and when I tried to talk to her about it, she just said it was all r-rubbish.'

'Hmm . . . well, maybe it'll surprise us, and things will get better with Sassy here,' said Hermione thoughtfully. 'I'm pretty sure Jessie actually likes her.'

At the adventure playground, Maggie rushed off to try all the exciting equipment, with Lucy following close behind to make sure she was safe. Hermione soon got bored and found herself wishing she'd brought a book to read. She wandered into the games building next to the playground and immediately laid eyes on Leo and some others playing table tennis. He was clowning around, balancing the racquet on his head as he walked back to the table after losing a point to Finn.

She watched them for a few seconds, and was about to slip out quickly when Finn spotted her and called out, 'Hey, Hermione! Wanna join us for the next match? Our friend is playing and we need a fourth for doubles – you can be on Leo's team.'

Leo dropped his clown act and waved sheepishly.

'Ermm, I . . .' Hermione tried to think of an excuse quickly, but her mind was blank. 'I'm not very good . . .' she started, nervously tucking a strand of hair behind her ear.

'Never mind that,' said Leo. 'I'm not exactly championship material myself.' He glanced quickly at her. 'But no worries if you don't want to.'

Hermione looked at his hopeful expression. 'Fine. But don't say I didn't warn you!' She laughed and picked up a racquet.

Twenty minutes later, the match was over and Hermione couldn't believe it – she and Leo had actually won!

'I'd better go. Lucy will be waiting,' she told him, slightly out of breath. 'Good match, guys,' she said cheerfully to the others.

'I'll walk you out,' offered Leo.

'Yes, mate!' hissed Finn encouragingly, and their friend Rafi leaned over and gave Leo a fist bump. Hermione hid a smile and pretended not to notice.

Leo pulled on a baseball cap as they stepped outside.

'Avoiding the sun?' said Hermione. 'I noticed you were a bit burned.'

Leo touched his nose self-consciously. 'Yeah . . . my nose is actually peeling. It's gross, I know.'

'No, it suits you,' said Hermione before she could stop herself. 'I mean – not the peeling bit –' Leo raised an eyebrow – 'just the, er, sunburn, brings some colour to your face.' She panicked. 'A healthy glow.'

A healthy glow?! she thought. It sounded like something from an Abby make-up tutorial. *Shoot me. Shoot me now.*

'Er, thanks . . . I think,' said Leo, grinning. 'So, like I was saying, did you know that the girl who plays Luna Lovegood was a Harry Potter superfan who went to an open call for auditions?'

Hermione laughed. 'Everyone knows that! Did you know she actually made the radish earrings she wore in *The Order of the Phoenix*?'

'No!'

'I nearly bought a pair off Etsy because they were so

cute. And a butterbeer cork necklace. You know, to—'

'Keep away Nargles!' They said at the same time.

Hermione felt her cheeks redden as she tried to think of something clever to say. 'Er, excellent knowledge there, Leo.' She noticed Lucy and Maggie waving to her from the playground. 'Wish I could chat more, but babysitting calls. See ya!' She waved to Leo and headed off, feeling a strange mix of relief and disappointment. She wondered if she would bump into him again.

'Did m-my eyes deceive me, or was that Leo p-paying you loads of attention?' teased Lucy affectionately as she approached. 'You've been gone ages!'

Hermione felt her cheeks flush again. 'Don't start. You know me – I'm a disaster with boys . . . but he's—'

'Oh, I-look! There's Sassy already!' exclaimed Lucy.

Hermione squinted. Even from a distance, it was possible to recognize her. She was getting out of her dad's car with all her gear. Her hair was a new shade of purple, and her outfit – a pink tulle skirt over leggings with Doc Martens – would have been more at home at a party than on a campsite.

They ran over to meet her.

Hermione could see Mr Lockwood do a double-take before he greeted Sassy's dad.

'Hey, Sass! So glad you're f-finally here!' said Lucy, and they all hugged.

While Sassy's father asked the Lockwoods a million questions about their plans for the week – nearest hospital, first-aid equipment, meals, etc. – Hermione and Lucy took Sassy into their tent so she could dump her stuff and see where she would sleep.

'This is so cool!' said Sassy, looking around.

When they got back outside, her dad was still talking to Mr Lockwood. 'OK, Dad, you can go now!' she urged.

'Can't wait to get rid of me,' he said, and laughed. 'Fine, but you must promise to obey Mr and Mrs Lockwood and, above all, stay safe. I want to hear from you every day, all right? Otherwise I'll be back here in a flash to see what's going on.'

Wow, thought Hermione, *he's almost as protective as Mum.*

'You got it, Dad!' said Sassy, and kissed him goodbye. 'Where are the others?' she asked as he got into his car and drove off.

'Down by the lake,' replied Lucy. 'I'll show you. H, are you c-coming?'

Hermione nodded. 'Yeah, let's get the whole gang together.' She glanced at Sassy's tutu. 'Er, just an idea, but you might want to change into something more . . . waterproof? We need to change too.'

Sassy grinned. 'Good point,' she said, and they all popped back into the tent.

After changing into her yellow one-shoulder swimsuit and wrapping a beach towel round her waist, Hermione quickly brushed her hair and swiped on some lipgloss, ignoring a questioning look from Lucy. She wanted to look nice . . . just in case.

Abby rushed over to give Sassy a hug when she saw her. 'Sa-sssssy!' she shrieked. 'Finally! Your bikini is absolute goals. And I love the hair . . .'

Hermione mimed covering her ears, raising a giggle from Jessie.

'Hey, welcome!' Jessie said to Sassy, giving her a high five.

There were dozens of people hanging out by the dock, some sunbathing, some splashing about in the lake with big inflatables. Hermione noticed that Leo and Finn were in the water along with the rest of their gang. Even though she'd hoped they would be there, she felt a rush of embarrassment and wondered if Leo thought she was stalking him.

'Are you coming in?' Finn called. 'We could all play Marco Polo.'

Hermione looked nervously at Abby, who rolled her eyes. 'They're only boys, H, nothing to be afraid of!'

'Abby, shut up!' hissed Hermione, dying inside. But then Leo gave her a wave from the water trampoline and she felt a bit better.

'Hey, guys,' called Abby confidently. 'Meet

Sassy, she's part of our squad.'

Hermione watched in awe as Sassy gave the boys a wave and then dived gracefully into the water near where they were swimming.

'I'm up for Marco Polo!' said Jessie, bombing off the dock and into the lake. She looked up, grinning and splashing. 'Are you guys coming?'

Lucy jumped in too, shortly followed by Abby. Hermione couldn't bear to be left alone on the dock, so she forced herself to jump in after them.

'Brrr, it's cold!' she exclaimed as she surfaced. She giggled as she caught sight of Leo's Bart Simpson shorts.

'I'll be it,' said Finn. He closed his eyes and counted to ten while the others swam away, but not too far. 'Marco!' he called out after reaching ten.

'Polo!' the others all shouted, and he started swimming towards their voices, trying to tag them.

'Marco!'

'Polo!' 'Polo!' 'Polo!' 'Polo!' they all replied in turn as they swam.

Leo suddenly broke the surface near to where Hermione was treading water. 'Hey!' he said, giving her a big smile. 'Long time no see!'

'I know, it's been too long,' she joked, relaxing instantly. 'I was beginning to forget what you looked like, actually.'

Out of the corner of her eye, she could see Abby nudging Lucy and pointing at her.

Whatever, she thought defiantly. *I don't care what they think. I'm just going to enjoy myself!*

She gave Leo a playful splash.

'You're it, H,' said Jessie, who had just swum up from behind and tagged her.

After they were all bored of playing Marco Polo, they moved over to the water inflatables. There was a huge trampoline and a raft with a slide off to one side as well as smaller inflatables, one in the shape of a cactus and one a pink flamingo. Jessie showed off some of her gymnastic moves on the trampoline, and Abby was choreographing some kind of intricate water ballet with Sassy.

'This trip is really fun,' said Hermione to Lucy, who had joined her on the big raft.

Leo had been entertaining her with Harry Potter film trivia until she'd got cramp in her leg and had to get out of the water. The girls lay back on their elbows, soaking up the sun.

'Thank you so much for inviting me,' she added.

'Oh, I'm just pleased you've made a new f-friend,' said Lucy, nodding in Leo's direction. He was attempting to sit on the flamingo while it bobbed up and down. 'He's cute.'

Hermione's happy mood ebbed a bit. 'Please, Luce, don't make a big thing out of this. I don't want to jinx anything, and let's not forget what a disaster my French hashtag *romance* was . . .'

Her experience with Thierry, the French boy she'd met on the school ski trip in the spring, had led to disappointment when she'd realized he just wanted to be friends. She had tried not to take it personally, but it had still been a blow to her already low self-confidence.

'Of course I w-won't embarrass you,' reassured Lucy.

'Hey, Hermione! Over here!' called Abby from the water.

Hermione looked over, and Abby and Sassy launched into a cheerleader chant. 'Give me an L! Give me an E!' they shouted.

'Oh my God, SHUT UP,' squealed Hermione, glancing at Leo, who was possibly within hearing distance.

'Give me an R!'

'I said shut – Wait, an R?'

'Give me an M! Give me an I! Give me an O! Give me an N! Give me an E . . . LERMIONE!'

'What the heck is Lermione?' asked Hermione in confusion. Then Lucy raised her eyebrows and it hit her.

'Guys, that is so lame!'

As Leo looked over, she panicked and jumped into the water, then swam off, a smile dancing on her lips.

VLOG 4

My Greatest Fear

7:35

FADE IN: BLACKWATER CAMPSITE.

LUCY, ABBY, JESSIE, HERMIONE and SASSY sitting round the
campfire at night, wearing cosy fleeces and holding cups of hot
chocolate. They all wave at the camera.

ALL
Hi, guys!

JESSIE

So tonight we thought we'd do a video about our greatest fears as the setting is nice and spooky . . . Can you hear the wind whistling in the trees? And just to get us started, I've got a little something here for Hermione!

JESSIE dangles a huge toy tarantula spider over HERMIONE's head. HERMIONE screams loudly and jumps up, knocking over her cup.

HERMIONE

EEEK! Ugh, it's disgusting!

JESSIE is laughing so hard she can barely talk

JESSIE

Calm down, it's fake, one of my brother's. You are SUCH an easy target!

JESSIE tries to hug her; HERMIONE resists.

HERMIONE

Not funny! And not cool when you know how I feel about

insects and creepy crawlies.

HERMIONE giggles a bit when JESSIE hugs her again.

HERMIONE (CONTINUED)

OK, OK, you're forgiven. So, yeah,
it should be obvious to everyone
now that my biggest fears are
insects and spiders. I don't like
snakes either, and I hate sharks,
which is why I don't like going in
deep water.

SASSY

Wow, that's like the entire animal kingdom! But those fears are

kinda understandable, and lots of people have them. I've got

a really random fear: I'm terrified of clowns and puppets and china dolls. I break out in a cold sweat when I see any of them.

ABBY

Really? How weird.

SASSY

It's something about them being almost human, but not. Like they're trying to trick me that they're friendly people, but I know they are actually evil.

(shudders)

Ugh.

JESSIE

Ha ha! What about you, Abs? You seem pretty fearless . . .

ABBY

I'm actually claustrophobic. I don't like being enclosed in small spaces. I'm always terrified of getting stuck in a lift, which is why I usually try to take the stairs.

SASSY

Oh, I thought that was a fitness kick, ha ha.

ABBY

No, I got stuck in a lift once, and I was there for ages before I got rescued. I thought I was going to die and started to have a panic attack. Eventually I started singing to myself, and it sorta calmed me down until they got me out.

LUCY

I would h-hate that too.

ABBY

Sometimes I get a bit panicky when I'm in a big crowd with everyone packed tightly together, especially if it's not moving. Like in a crush on the underground. I'm worried that I won't be able to escape.

JESSIE

Scary. Luce, are you afraid of anything?

LUCY

Not much . . . I love all k-kinds of animals, even the ones with

h-hundreds of legs . . . but I s-suppose I do have that very

b-basic fear . . . which is that I'm afraid of the d-dark. Well, not

really the dark . . . but what might be lurking in the d-dark.

JESSIE

(mischievously)

Like an axe murderer?

LUCY

Yeah, sort of! I don't like f-footsteps behind me in the dark.

HERMIONE

But that's just common sense. Being afraid of the dark is like an

evolutionary fear. I mean, that's why cavemen made fires and

why we have lights indoors. And why we have this campfire

today! OK, Jessie, what about
you then?

JESSIE

I'm not keen on axe murderers
either.
(grins)
But the only thing I'm really terrified of is needles – as in,
injections.
(shivers)
Stupid, I know, because they make you healthier. I just can't
stand looking at the needle pierce the skin.

ABBY

I'm guessing you won't ever get any tattoos then!
(to camera)
We'd love to hear what you guys might be frightened of . . .
so comment down below and let us know. For now, we're all
feeling safe and cosy round the fire . . .

HERMIONE

Even though my hot chocolate got spilt because of Jessie!

ALL

Bye!

FADE OUT.

Views: 11,282

Subscriptions: 26,002

Comments:

ShyGirl1: I can't stand people being sick around me!

anonymouse: i am scared of buttons. weird but true, all my clothes have zips and Velcro . . .

sami_rules: cats. they are sooo sinister, especially when they purr really loudly. It's like, what are you plotting??

xxrainbowxx: balloons – well i have a fear of them popping

queen_dakota: my fear is boring videos made by losers.

jazzyjessie [reply to queen_dakota]: just a friendly tip – stop watching them then!!!

(scroll down to see 49 more comments)

Chapter Five: Jessie

It was the middle of the night, and there was a storm raging, thunder rumbling around the campsite, and lightning cracking overhead.

Jessie was unfazed.

'Perfect occasion for pick and mix,' she said happily. She felt like Bear Grylls toughing it out on a deserted island somewhere.

The sides of the tent shook as the wind howled outside.

'Hngghh!' cried Hermione, scooching down into her sleeping bag. 'This is scary. We're like Dorothy in the tornado. I keep expecting the tent to blow away!'

Jessie checked the tent pegs and glanced at the roof. 'We're fine and, most importantly, no leaks. Have a fizzy worm,' she ordered, patting Hermione's feet reassuringly.

Everyone grabbed a handful of sweets and huddled up together. It was quite crowded with Sassy there now too, but eventually they got back to sleep.

In the morning, there were puddles on the ground, but it was sunny.

'Hurry up, girls,' said Lucy's mum over breakfast. 'We're off to the seaside today.'

'Is today surfing?' gasped Jessie. *Finally!*

'Yes,' confirmed Mrs Lockwood. 'I've got to check out the seal sanctuary at Princeton Point, and I'll drop you off at the watersports school in Maxwell's Bay. Maggie and Dad will stay here and go fishing.'

'I'm gonna find Nemo!' said Maggie, her eyes wide with excitement.

Jessie laughed. 'Good luck with that, Mags.' As she finished another pancake, she joined in with Lucy's dad who had starting singing 'Surfing USA' by the Beach Boys . . . She was hyped!

The drive to the seaside was fun. The music was on loud, and they all continued singing loudly. Abby was filming them the whole time. Since Sassy had arrived, Jessie had noticed Abby dragging her away every time they got the opportunity to talk, but . . . whatever! Jessie was determined to enjoy today's adventure.

The approach to Maxwell's Bay was along a winding cliff road, and the sea was shimmering turquoise way down below. When they finally reached the fishing village, with its picturesque white houses and tiny lanes, everyone gasped. There was a small harbour with cafes and shops and swooping seagulls.

'It's so cute!' exclaimed Hermione. 'Just like an old-fashioned postcard. I bet there's a wonderful bakery, and a dusty old bookshop with a resident cat. Maybe I should stay here while you all go surfing.'

'No, H, you are c-coming with us!' Lucy laughed. 'But, speaking of postcards, I should send one to Sam. I m-miss him loads.'

'Nah, we'll be home by the time he gets it,' said Abby. 'I'm not bothering for Charlie.'

'There's the watersports school!' cried Jessie, pointing at a bright orange sign. Her brothers Leon and Jake were going to be so jealous! She led the way, and they all hurried into the office to sign up.

'Bad news, girls,' said Mrs Lockwood, once she'd spoken to the manager. 'The surfboards have all been rented out today.'

'Oh well, bookshops and bakeries it is,' said Hermione happily.

Jessie's heart sank, and it must have shown on her face.

'Don't despair, Jess!' said Mrs Lockwood. 'The manager is suggesting that you try SUP lessons instead. They have plenty of equipment for that. Are you up for it?'

'Totally!' said Jessie, perking up again. 'I've seen SUP on YouTube. It's really popular in America.'

'Yeah, Morgan's sent me videos of her d-doing it,' agreed Lucy. 'It looks great.'

'What's SUP?' asked Hermione reluctantly.

'Good one, H,' Jessie quipped, and they all laughed.

'No, I mean it,' said Hermione, sounding slightly embarrassed. 'I don't know.'

'Stand-up paddleboarding,' Jessie explained.

'I think it's actually easier to l-learn than getting up on a surfboard,' added Lucy.

Hermione started to look less anxious.

'Let's do it, guys!' said Sassy, looking at the photos in the office.

'Will your dad be OK with you doing this, Sassy, or do you want me to call him?' asked Mrs Lockwood. 'I told him you'd be trying surfing, but not this, and he wanted to be kept posted of every activity.'

Jessie hummed impatiently while they decided to text Sassy's father and await his reply. Then, FINALLY, it was time to hit the waves!

Their teacher was a really cool Australian woman with dreadlocks called Razzy. Jessie mentally added 'watersports instructor' to her list of dream jobs. (The list also included gymnast, professional prankster and video-game designer.)

'The sea's quite warm here in the harbour cos it's shallow and sheltered, so I don't think you need wet suits. You should be fine in board shorts over your swimsuits.' She handed out the shorts, and Jessie grabbed a grey-and-turquoise pair. 'And life vests, of course. Don't forget to put some sunscreen on. I'll be back in a moment.'

The girls slathered on the sunscreen, and Razzy returned with the life vests.

'OK,' she began, 'so we'll just practise on the beach for a few minutes before we get in the water. You can carry the board by the handle in the middle. Although the water here is very calm, it's still a good idea to use the leash round your ankle so that the board can't float away from you. You just fasten it with the Velcro.' Razzy demonstrated on her own board. 'Then you start off on your knees in the middle of the board on either side of the handle. When you're comfortable and ready to stand up, you pop your paddle across the board in front of you, tuck your toes under and bring your legs up to standing, one at a time. Then start paddling straight away as it will help you keep your balance.'

The girls carried their boards down to the beach and practised getting up from a kneeling position to standing.

'This is easy!' pronounced Jessie, once she'd done it a couple of times. She looked around eagerly. 'Let's hit the waves!'

'Shall we give it a go, then?' asked Razzy. 'Is everyone else ready?'

'I think so,' said Abby uncertainly.

'Whoop, whoop!' cried Sassy.

They waded out into the water. It was a bit chilly at first, but Jessie soon got used to it.

'OK, up on your knees, then just start paddling,' called Razzy. 'I want you to feel really comfortable doing that before you stand up.'

But Jessie had already jumped up to standing position, and she was filming using the GoPro attached to her head. It felt so natural to her.

'How are you doing that, Jess?' Sassy asked admiringly.

'Raw talent!' said Jessie with a grin. 'And, OK, maybe my gymnastics training has something to do with it . . . It's all about finding your balance.'

The others were just getting used to moving around, and Abby kept crashing into them and giggling.

Jessie forged ahead, the water calm on either side of her. 'By the way, how do I stop?' she called as the others became smaller and smaller behind her.

'Jump in the water!' Razzy laughed. 'No, just use your paddle as a brake.'

'Looking amazing out there!' called Sassy.

Jessie paddled around while the others knelt in the distance, she could hear Abby swearing under her breath as her knees slid off the board.

After a few minutes, Razzy said, 'OK, let's try

standing up, everyone else. Put your paddle in front of you, tuck your toes under and stand up! Good, Lucy, and you too, Sassy. Look in front of you and start paddling. Abby, you're standing too far forward, you're going to—'

SPLASH!

'N-not again, Abs!' Lucy laughed.

Abby spat out a mouthful of water and tried to clamber back on to the board.

Jessie opened her mouth to make a joke about wannabe mermaids and stopped herself, seeing the slightly frustrated expression on Abby's face. Maybe it was better to keep quiet.

'OK, Abby, the worst has already happened,' said Razzy, 'and it wasn't so bad – was it? Take your time and try again. Watch Jessie's technique.'

Soon everyone was up on their boards apart from Hermione, chatting as they paddled.

'This is way better than surfing,' said Jessie, 'cos you can talk while you're doing it.'

'Well, we all know you can't control yourself with that!' remarked Abby.

Jessie looked over at her in shock – where had that come from? And since when was Jessie any more chatty than Abby?

She didn't know what to say – and neither did anyone else. They all paddled in silence for a few seconds.

Then Hermione said, 'Jess, can you come here? I wanna try standing up now. Can you help me?'

Relieved to have something to do other than be snapped at by Abby, Jessie paddled over and managed to get Hermione up on the board.

Razzy went back to the shore, and the girls continued mucking around on the SUPs, but the mood had changed, and Jessie ended up paddling around by herself for the final half hour.

Later, when their time was up and they were getting tired and cold – 'Guaranteed I won't be doing that again,' said Abby as she wrapped herself in a towel – they headed off to the harbour and found a cafe with some outside seating.

Jessie was buzzing from her new favourite sport. She'd interviewed Razzy for the channel and was really proud of how it had gone. Now she was famished.

'My idea of heaven,' she said as she tucked into a large portion of chips.

'Mine too,' echoed Sassy. Suddenly she shrieked. A huge gull had swooped down and snatched a chip right out of her hands.

'OMG!' exclaimed Hermione. 'That came out of nowhere – it was like the Hungarian Horntail that Harry has to battle in the Triwizard Tournament!'

Jessie laughed. 'Of course it was.'

'Amazing!' said Abby, who had been filming. 'Oh, sorry, Sassy, are you OK?'

'Yeah, it just took me by surprise,' she replied.

Jessie watched the seagull pecking its reward, then noticed some boys jumping from the harbour wall into the sea. It was quite a long drop.

'That looks cool,' she said, her eyes lighting up. 'I might give it a go.'

'Oh, please d-don't!' cried Lucy. 'It's s-so d-dangerous.'

'No, Jess, you mustn't,' said Hermione. 'What if something happened? It wouldn't be fair to Lucy's parents . . .'

'Exactly,' said Abby curtly. 'Maybe you should try thinking of someone else for a change.'

'What are you talking about?' asked Jessie. Why did Abby keep attacking her? 'When do I . . . Abby, I don't understand.'

'Well, with all your pranks and making us eat weird stuff and go kayaking and extreme sports . . . sometimes maybe you should just chill out a bit. Be more normal.'

'What, and spend my time like you, shopping and trying on outfits?' snapped Jessie angrily. She could see from the expression on Abby's face that she'd hit a nerve, but she didn't care any more. She'd had enough of being on the receiving end of Abby's weird comments. 'Jeez, it's not my fault you have a worse sense of balance than a drunk person walking the plank.'

'Guys, please,' said Hermione anxiously. 'I think we're all just super tired; let's chill out and wait for Lucy's mum to pick us up. Maybe an ice cream while we wait?'

'Fine,' said Abby, looking at her phone.

'Fine,' said Jessie. She wasn't sure she wanted to be here any more.

After another barbecue dinner, Lucy and Abby did the washing-up while Lucy's parents did bedtime with Maggie in the tent.

Jessie was dreading the GCV meeting they had planned for the evening. The tension between her and Abby was going to make things really difficult. It was OK when Lucy's parents and Maggie were around, but when it was just the five of them, there was nowhere to hide.

'Jess?'

Jessie looked up from her black, incinerated marshmallow at Abby who was coming over to her spot by the campfire.

'Washing-up's done. Can we . . . talk . . . before the meeting?'

Jessie shrugged. 'OK.'

Abby looked uncomfortable. 'Like, OK, so there's obviously a problem between us, and I honestly don't know where it's come from. But Lucy was just saying that sometimes I can sound sharper than I really want to? And that it's upsetting for you?' She avoided Jessie's eye.

Jessie swallowed. She hated confrontation, and this was so, so awkward. 'Well – yeah. I guess I feel like you've been kind of harsh to me ever since the City Farm thing, and that video.' She paused. 'And . . . I know you really like Sassy, which we all do, but it's like you don't have much respect for me any more.' There. She'd said it.

'What?' said Abby. 'That's crazy! Don't be so dramatic.'

Jessie sighed, poking the fire with her skewer. Abby really didn't take criticism well. 'Fine, but you asked if you'd been upsetting me, and I'm just saying, yeah, I guess you have been. So now maybe I'm being a little harsh back, not that I'm trying to score points.' She looked up. Abby was braiding her hair over one shoulder and looking into the distance. Jessie didn't know what else to say.

Eventually Abby said, 'OK, fine. Sorry if I offended you. I obviously think you're great, but not always a hundred per cent interested in GCV . . . Like, sometimes you act a little bored with us.'

Jessie tried to protest, but Abby spoke over her.

'Well, even if you're not . . . you have a load of other interests.'

Jessie shrugged. So what if she did? Was Abby somehow jealous of her hobbies?

'And because Sassy is a new member, she just seems a lot more . . . excited, I guess.'

'OK,' said Jessie slowly. 'But you shouldn't think I don't love our group. Cos I do.'

'Fine,' said Abby. 'Speaking of which, shall we put this behind us and get on with the meeting? I have news!'

Jessie almost laughed. She loved the channel, but

it was true nobody loved it as fiercely as Abby. And she guessed this was as close to an apology as she was going to get, although Abby still hadn't apologized for the City Farm vlog. *Be the bigger person*, as her dad liked to say.

'Yes, Abs, let's get on with the meeting.'

'Awesome,' said Abby with obvious relief. 'OK, guys, gather round . . . Let's get this show on the road!' she called.

The others came and joined them, and Lucy glanced questioningly at Jessie, who smiled, letting her know things were OK, for now at least.

'First,' said Abby gleefully. 'I've been dying to tell you guys all evening . . . but thought I should wait for the meeting.'

'Drama queen!' said Lucy. 'W-what is it?'

Abby spoke fast. 'Tiffany texted me. She knows we're going to Chesterbury and has arranged for us to do something cool there, through one of her contacts at this local radio station.'

Jessie gasped – for once, the news lived up to Abby's drama!

'Really?' she asked. 'What is it?'

'It's a fashion segment for the radio station – interviewing people at the festival about their outfits.' She looked around. 'If it's OK with you guys, I'd really like to be the one to do it.'

'That d-does sound like it's perfect for you, Abs,' said Lucy.

'Yeah, I wouldn't know what to ask!' said Hermione.

Sassy nodded, and Jessie had to admit she felt the same too, even though she was still a bit jealous at the same time. Now she understood why Abby had been in a better mood this evening.

'Amazing. I'll tell Tiffany,' said Abby happily. 'I'll still need help rounding up people to interview and stuff, so it will be a group effort, and the main thing is I'll get a chance to plug our channel.' She glanced down at her notebook. 'Moving on. Let's talk about vlog content for the rest of this trip. I know Jessie's taken some cool footage with the GoPro of the SUPing, plus the Razzy interview, but we still need to think of more to inspire us.'

Jessie chewed on a fresh marshmallow. She was tempted to suggest a complicated prank, but she was still sensitive about suggesting that after Abby's comment earlier.

'Well, the f-festival will be pretty amazing to film,' said Lucy.

'True,' said Abby, 'and we need to plan that carefully, but I meant something else as well . . . something completely different to anything we've ever done before.'

'I know!' exclaimed Sassy. 'I have the perfect idea . . . let's make a scary movie.'

Jessie sat up.

'Here in the forest,' continued Sassy. 'We can make it really creepy – film it in the woods at night and then edit it with music and special effects when we get home.'

Jessie grinned. This sounded AWESOME.

'I like it . . . but we don't want to make it too gruesome,' said Abby, looking pensive. 'We've got our younger viewers to think about.'

'We could make it more mysterious than scary,' suggested Hermione.

'Yeah, and put some silly bits in, to lighten the tone,' added Jessie, ideas already popping into her head. In some ways a scary movie was like an elaborate prank . . . on the audience.

Abby was nodding. 'Well it's definitely different . . . Lucy, are you in?'

Lucy grinned. 'Completely.'

As Jessie got ready for bed, she felt unexpectedly happy that Sassy had joined them. This movie was going to be SERIOUSLY FUN, way more interesting than looking at people's outfits! She went to sleep that night thinking of fake blood and blurry camera angles.

VLOG 5

SUP-ing and Stuff

12:48

FADE IN: THE BEACH,

JESSIE filming herself on her phone, standing on her SUP board on the beach.

JESSIE

Hi, guys! So today we're having a day of watersports at Maxwell's Bay, and I thought I'd try to catch a bit of the SUP vibe on film. I'll be using my phone and a GoPro, so the quality might not be great, but at least it's authentic!

MONTAGE: JESSIE, LUCY, ABBY, HERMIONE and SASSY all practising on the beach.

JESSIE
(voiceover)
First we practise a bit here on the beach – how to stand up and the best way to paddle – and then we're out on the water. Can't wait!

JESSIE filming on GoPro so we see ABBY, LUCY, SASSY and HERMIONE on their paddleboards in the water.

JESSIE
Isn't this cool?

ABBY
I could just lie out here and get a tan. Or do my nails . . .

SASSY

I think some people do yoga routines and stuff out on their
paddleboards.

JESSIE

H? How you doing?

HERMIONE

OK, I guess. It's not as scary as I thought it would be. Our
instructor Razzy's been very reassuring . . .

SASSY

(shouting)

Look out, H! There's a dark shape coming up behind you . . .
Dun dun dun dun dun dun dun dun . . .

HERMIONE shrieks and looks round anxiously.

HERMIONE

What? What is it? Where?

SASSY

(laughing)

Gotcha!

JESSIE

Moving on! How about a race? We could go out to that buoy a bit further out in the harbour?

ABBY

(annoyed)

Why are you so full of beans?

Can't you just laze about like the rest of us?

LUCY

Come on, Abs! L-let's do it!

HERMIONE

I'll stay here and be the referee. Ready, steady, go!

Suddenly we see the front of the paddleboard and paddle

moving quickly through the water. The film is from the POV of JESSIE's GoPro strapped to her head. Lots of shrieking and laughing. Suddenly a big splash. JESSIE's GoPro turns and films ABBY, who has fallen in the water.

ABBY
Argh! Not again!

HERMIONE
(shouting)
Go, Luce! You can do it!

JESSIE's GoPro shows another paddleboard coming into view alongside JESSIE. It's LUCY paddling hard. With a big stroke, she pulls ahead of JESSIE and reaches the buoy first.

ABBY, SASSY and HERMIONE
(shout together)
Result! Hooray! You won!

JESSIE

Well, done, Luce! You really pulled it out of the bag!

LUCY

(laughing)

I'm knackered! Now, I'm j-just gonna chill.

CUT TO: JESSIE and RAZZY back on shore.

RAZZY

So you really seem to have taken to this like a duck to water!

(laughs)

Excuse the corny expression. You've got a good sense of balance.

JESSIE

Well, I love sports: gymnastics, snowboarding, skateboarding . . .

I was really hoping to try surfing today – it looks so cool.

RAZZY

Yes, sorry about that, but I'm sure you'll get another chance. I think you'd be good at it and learn quickly.

JESSIE

So how did you get to be here? Sorry if that sounds nosy.

RAZZY

(laughs)

No worries. Well, I'm from Australia, and I began

bodyboarding as a little kid. Then I started surfing in my early

teens, so I've been doing it for years!

JESSIE

How do you become an instructor?

RAZZY

Well, there's a course with a qualification. You need lots of

experience surfing, but you also have to be very fit. You have to

pass a beach lifeguard course, which includes first aid.

JESSIE

But you did that in Australia. Are you able to work anywhere?

RAZZY

Yeah, the qualification is recognized internationally, so I've been travelling around the world, teaching as I go. I've been to Bali, New Zealand, Hawaii, and now I'm in England for the summer.

JESSIE

What an awesome way to live! I'd love to do that!

RAZZY

I can't complain – it's a great lifestyle.

JESSIE

So what's the best part of the job?

RAZZY

Meeting lots of people, travelling the world, being outside in the elements, doing what I love.

JESSIE

And the worst?

RAZZY

The water in the UK can get a bit . . . chilly, and there's a short surfing season here, but I tend to just move on to somewhere warmer. I'm heading off to South Africa in October.

JESSIE

I'd love to have your life! You're so lucky.

RAZZY

(laughing)

There's nothing special about me. You could do it if you wanted to, I'm sure. It's all about having the courage to live your dreams.

JESSIE

Thanks, Razzy, this has been so inspiring! OK, guys, so that's it from us at Maxwell's Bay. If any of you have been surfing or SUPing, let us know in the comments down below! And give us a thumbs-up if you enjoyed this video.

FADE OUT.

Views: 12,011

Subscribers: 26,499

Comments:

PrankingsteinJosh: so cool!

girlscanvlogfan: looking great out there, Jessie xx

funny internetperson54: Razzy is hotttttt!

miavlogs: you guys are always trying new things together, it's so inspiring ❤️

letsgosurfing: paddle over to my channel and watch some of my surfing vlogs!

MagicMorgan: Stoked that you guys are SUP-ers now!

Anyadoesthesplits: Fantastic Jessie!

Chapter Six: Sassy

'Right, let's get to work,' said Sassy as they all sat round the picnic table with cups of coffee the following morning. Mr and Mrs Lockwood had taken Maggie back to the adventure playground after breakfast, and Sassy felt kind of relieved as she still didn't know them that well. It was always slightly intimidating getting to know your friends' parents, even though the Lockwoods seemed friendly.

Sassy felt really pumped about her video idea. Over the last few years, she'd loved growing her channel, SassySays, which now had 5,000 subscribers. She didn't make any one particular kind of video, just whatever sparked her imagination and whatever she thought her viewers would enjoy. She'd been so excited to join the Girls Can Vlog channel a couple of months ago because it gave her the opportunity to work with a group. She loved doing collabs and bouncing ideas off other people.

The girls all seemed really nice too, and she'd never had a friendship 'group' before, not that she had opened up to them about that. She'd noticed some tension between Abby and Jessie, but as of last night it seemed like that situation had blown over. Abby had told her to take the lead on the scary movie, and she was raring to go. She was eager to prove she could do something more original than stupid lipstick challenges.

'We have some decisions to make, and then we can start planning,' she began, sounding more confident than she felt. 'First of all, we need to decide what sort of film we want to make—'

'I love monster and alien movies,' interrupted Jessie. 'They're my faves cos they're scary but also funny.'

'Yeah, but then you need costumes, which we don't have here,' pointed out Sassy. She didn't want to shoot down anyone's ideas too soon, but she thought Jessie would be cool about this.

'True,' agreed Jessie. 'That can be our next movie, once we're back home.'

'Perfect!' said Sassy happily.

'Maybe we could film a story that's about somewhere haunted . . . sort of ghostly and mysterious,' suggested Hermione.

'Sounds good,' said Sassy. She knew Hermione was a huge bookworm and book tuber, so she would probably have loads of ideas for a mysterious setting. 'Everyone agree?'

They all nodded.

Sassy sipped her coffee. 'The next step is the most important, and I think you'll be great at it, Hermione: we need a good story. Our setting is here in the woods, but what's going to happen and who are the characters?'

'Scary films always start with a happy, normal-looking situation,' said Abby.

Everyone nodded and tried to think of ideas.

'So it could be a camping trip, like ours, which goes

wrong,' began Hermione tentatively. 'There's something dodgy lurking in a haunted place.'

'What would the haunted place be?' asked Sassy, taking notes on her phone. 'Maybe the toilet blocks?'

'The ghost of last night's curry!' Jessie giggled.

'The ghost of s-someone who got locked in the toilet – that would be fun!' said Lucy.

'Nooo!' said Abby. 'That actually happened to me once at school, when Kayleigh locked me in a toilet backstage at the theatre. Waaay too close to home!'

'Oh yeah!' said Lucy. 'Sorry, I forgot. That was s-so out of order!'

They all laughed, and Sassy started to feel a tiny bit left out until Lucy continued, 'We'll have to tell you the f-full story some time.'

She nodded gratefully. 'Sounds like one I definitely need to hear.'

'Dakota was behind it, as usual!' said Hermione. 'Just

you wait till you meet her – you'll see what we've all been dealing with.'

Sassy groaned. 'She's bad enough on her YouTube channel, not sure if I could cope IRL.' Dakota came across as a total nightmare. She glanced back at her notes. 'OK, so . . . not the toilet, then.'

'What about the boathouse?' suggested Hermione. 'It could be haunted by someone who kept falling off their kayak.' She glanced coyly at Abby.

'Mean!' said Abby, a smile spreading over her face. 'But I like it! So we need a reason for them to go into the boathouse at night.'

'Who are the characters?' asked Jessie.

'Well,' said Sassy, 'usually there's a main character with a sidekick or two. The main character is often impulsive and foolhardy, so they head straight for danger. They have to be likeable, though, so you care about what happens to them. Then they've usually got a friend who's more reluctant and cautious, who warns them not to go, and stuff like that.'

'Too bad we don't have a dog like in *Scooby Doo*,' joked Jessie. 'Abs, you should have brought Weenie.'

'Ha ha – can you imagine his little face?' Abby giggled. 'So, who's going to play the main character?' she asked, looking hopeful.

'Let's get the story sorted before we get into casting,' replied Sassy quickly, avoiding the question. She knew that Abby loved acting, but she didn't know if she should automatically get the lead role. Sassy actually had someone else in mind.

'Maybe we have two girls on a camping trip who are making a film about some mystery,' Hermione said, getting into her stride.

She looked so cute, her face the picture of concentration. Sassy could totally picture her as an author in front of an old-fashioned typewriter, tapping out her next bestseller.

'Perhaps,' continued Hermione, her face lighting up, 'their older sister disappeared mysteriously years ago at the lake, and they've come back to try to find out what happened. They're both kind of incompetent – that's where the humour comes in.'

'S-someone needs to warn them not to go to the l-lake and especially not the b-boathouse. It could be some old man at the shop or a caretaker . . . or some really over-the-top scary m-music . . . but, anyway, they need to be warned,' added Lucy.

'So there are lots of warnings, but then something needs to make them go anyway,' summed up Sassy.

'Maybe there's a thunderstorm and they have to shelter in the boathouse?' suggested Hermione.

'Yes!' said Sassy, high-fiving her across the table. 'Hermione, I could kiss you!'

It took them a couple of hours to work out the storyline, and by the time they had finished, the Lockwoods had returned. They'd tried to drag the girls out to the lake, and had been sent packing. So they'd gone out again and left them to it, setting the girls up with some snacks and drinks and warning them to stay in the shade as the day was hotting up quickly.

Sassy was buzzing with how good the story was. 'Now we should make a storyboard – it can be really rough – but just to plan what we are filming scene by scene,' she said, opening a packet of crisps. She ate one then gestured around with the second one. 'We should plan some jump scares in a few key places, but not too many or they'll have less impact.'

'What's a j-jump scare?' asked Lucy.

'Oh, I know that from video games,' replied Jessie. 'It's when you scare the audience by surprising them with a quick change of image, usually together with a loud, frightening sound, right? Something that makes them jump with fear.'

'Exactly,' said Sassy.

'So what about the music and sound effects?' asked Abby.

'We'll do that later when we're editing back home. We'll be able to plan it carefully to really enhance the filming. There are websites where we can get free music and sound effects like footsteps and heavy breathing, and maybe some canned laughter too, for the funny bits.'

'And what about lighting?' asked Hermione. 'We're filming at night, but we only have our torches and some lanterns. How's that going to work?'

'I think it's a f-full moon,' said Lucy. 'That sh-should help.'

'We'll need to use a lens opening for shooting in low light and we should try to light our subjects from behind,' replied Sassy, thinking back to the videos she'd watched.

'Wow, someone's done their homework!' said Hermione.

Tired and sweaty after their morning's work, they took a break for lunch and went down to the dock for a swim. The boys weren't there, as they'd gone off on a day trip, but the girls had fun messing about on the inflatables. That was until Sassy started thinking about the movie again . . . It was taking over her brain – it was going to be the coolest thing ever!

After their swim, Sassy bought them all slushies. 'OK, so back to work, guys,' she said as she handed the bright pink and blue drinks round. 'We need to cast the parts and decide who's doing what. I'd really like to do the main filming. I hope that's OK with everyone?'

'Makes sense,' said Hermione, 'because you're the director and you have a vision for the film.'

The others nodded, and Sassy smiled gratefully.

'Thanks, guys. Next, I'd really like Abby to help with the lighting, which will need to be done during the filming,' continued Sassy.

Abby looked momentarily disappointed, but nodded in agreement.

'Also, Abs, I'd like you to do the make-up of the ghost of Ghost Girl. I hope you brought some products with you!'

'Never go anywhere without my make-up!' Abby laughed. 'And I did bring quite a lot for Chesterbury.'

Sassy was relieved. She'd expected Abby to throw a tantrum about not playing the lead.

'So that leaves Lucy, Jessie and Hermione to play the various parts,' Sassy continued.

'I really don't want to be in this,' said Hermione. 'I know I'll be rubbish.' She smiled apologetically at Sassy. 'Ask anyone. I'm no good at acting.'

'Well, you can be the ghost who doesn't say anything but just looks creepy,' said Sassy, smiling. 'And makes them laugh – Ghost Girl should be soaking wet with mascara running down her face.'

'You can d-do that, H,' said Lucy encouragingly. 'Come on.'

'No problem for you to look frightening!' joked Jessie.

Hermione shoved her. 'Well, maybe . . . if I don't have to speak,' said Hermione reluctantly.

'Jessie, I think you'd make a great lead,' suggested Sassy, 'and you, Luce, can be her friend. How does that sound?'

'Cool!' said Jessie.

They started filming the daytime shots that afternoon: arriving at the campsite with its sign, panning shots of the dark woods and lake, and even a shot of the camp caretaker in front of the boathouse. Sassy persuaded him to stand leaning on his broom scowling at the camera.

'Terrific!' she said, and thanked him. 'You'll be famous!'

Over supper they talked excitedly about what they'd been doing with Lucy's parents.

'It sounds very impressive,' said Lucy's dad. 'And very creative.'

'Will you be filming more this evening?' asked Lucy's mum.

'Yeah, we need to do the night scenes,' replied Sassy. 'We'll need to use the lanterns, if that would be OK?' she asked politely.

'Sure,' said Lucy's dad. 'But I want you to be extra careful in the dark, and no going out on the water for this Ghost Girl. Understood?'

'No fear!' said Hermione.

'And I want you back by ten at the latest,' said Lucy's mum.

The actors went to get ready in the tent. Sassy supervised as Abby put some make-up on Jessie and Lucy, and then she got to work on turning Hermione into a damp and annoyed-looking ghost. She put on thick white foundation and made Hermione's eyes very dark so that they looked hollow. Then she applied deep red lipstick and mascara streaks, plus a couple of fake spots, before drenching her with a jug of water over the head.

'Whoa!' exclaimed Jessie. 'She looks amazing – you're kind of scary and pitiful at the same time, Hermione.'

'That's f-fantastic, Abs,' said Lucy.

Even Hermione smiled when she looked in the mirror. 'Let's hope I don't bump into Leo tonight, ha ha.'

'Good job, Abby,' praised Sassy, feeling pumped.

'Now, are we ready to roll?'

They trudged off into the woods with their lanterns and headed down towards the boathouse. The moon was rising over the lake, and it all looked perfect.

'Lights, camera, action!' called Abby, who was assisting, and Sassy started to film.

All too soon it was 10 p.m. and they went back to the campsite, laughing and talking non-stop. They snacked on popcorn and drank the expensive cocoa Lucy's mum had made them.

There'd been lots of giggling, screaming, running and falling down clumsily, and Jessie had been hilarious as a scared teenager about to wet herself when she first saw Hermione's ghostly face appear.

'I just wish we'd got more done.' Sassy sighed. 'With the retakes, it all eats up more time than I'd thought. There's so much left to do.'

'We still have tomorrow night,' reassured Abby.

'I'm knackered,' said Jessie. 'I need to crash.'

They took off their make-up, brushed their teeth and

were soon in their sleeping bags.

But Sassy found she couldn't sleep. She lay in her sleeping bag thinking of all the shots she hadn't managed to film and bursting with new ideas.

Then there was a low rumble of thunder from an incoming storm. Suddenly Sassy saw a flash of lightning through the opening of the tent.

This would be perfect for the film . . .

VLOG 6

FADE IN: Night-time. SASSY, wrapped up in a hoody, jeans, big scarf and hat, filming herself in the woods. She lights up her chin with a torch.

SASSY

Hi, guys. We've been filming our scary movie all afternoon, and now we're about to do the night-time scenes, when things get really grisly, mwa ha ha. Not really; it's all kind of ridiculous, actually! We'll post the full video when it's edited and we've

added all the effects in and stuff, but in the meantime we
wanted to give you a little sneak preview and take you along
for some of the filming. No spoilers, though, I promise! So to
clue you in . . . Jessie and Lucy are two ditsy twin sisters, Milly
and Rachel. Their older sister, Flora, disappeared several years
ago on a camping trip, and now that they're old enough to
investigate, they've returned to the place where it happened.
Little do they know that Flora IS here . . . but not as they
remember her. She's not as sweet as she used to be, and she's
a LOT soggier! OK, Jessie, Lucy, here we go . . .

SASSY pans over the sky so we can see the full moon.

SASSY
Lights, camera, action . . .

She turns the camera to film JESSIE
and LUCY walking through the
woods.

JESSIE

(loud Australian accent)

I just know she's still out here somewhere.

LUCY bursts out laughing.

SASSY

CUT!

LUCY

Sorry, but why d-did you do that accent, Jess?! You weren't

Australian in the earlier s-scenes.

JESSIE

Ha ha, no idea! It just came out. Must have been Razzy's

influence. Will try again.

SASSY

Take two.

JESSIE

I just know she's still out here somewhere.

LUCY

(exaggerated sniffing)

I d-don't know where this hunch is coming from, Milly. Are you

sure? It's fr-freezing out here tonight. And so, so dark . . .

JESSIE and LUCY both jump.

LUCY (CONTINUED)

W-what was that?

JESSIE

Just an owl. Trust me, OK, Rachel?

Everything's fine. And we have to do

this! Otherwise we'll never know what

happened.

LUCY looks up at the trees moving in the wind.

LUCY

F-fine, but there's a storm coming. What
if we get s-struck by lightning? It will
p-play havoc with my hair!

JESSIE

OK, let's shelter in the boathouse for a while.

LUCY

(sniffing)

Isn't it s-supposed to be h-haunted?

JESSIE

You don't believe those old tales, do
you? There's nothing to be afraid of.

SASSY

And CUT! Well done, guys. We'll add the owl noise in later.

CUT TO: The boathouse. It's pitch black so we can only hear their voices.

LUCY

H-hello, is someone there?

JESSIE

Hello?

(Silence . . .)

JESSIE

(screams)

What was that?

HERMIONE

OW! You whacked me in the leg!

SASSY

CUT! Hermione, we're not meant to hear from you yet! In fact, we don't hear from you at all – no lines, remember!

HERMIONE

Aghh, well, can't we switch a light on so we can see where we're going?

SASSY

(with a sigh)

No. Let's take it from the top . . .

CUT TO: Outside the boathouse.

JESSIE and LUCY running away from the boathouse, brandishing a torch.

LUCY

I t-told you this was a b-bad idea!
Let's g-get out of here before it's too l-late!

JESSIE

AAAH! HELP! It's behind us!

LUCY

RUNNNNN!

We see a figure dressed in black with a ghostly white face and damp hair running behind them.

FADE OUT.

Views: 18,732

Subscribers: 27,489

Comments:

miavlogs: when Jessie did that accent!

sami_rules: That make-up, guys!!! hahahaha

girlscanvlogfan: Can't wait to see the finished movie! You

guys are so talented xx

Sammylovesbooks: was that Hermione at the end?

queen_dakota: Lol this is super lame.

PrankingsteinCharlie: So cool. Can't wait to see the real thing.

(scroll down to see 25 more comments)

Chapter Seven:
Lucy

Lucy was being chased by something very frightening that was just behind her. She heard heavy breathing . . . She fell to the ground, but managed to scramble up again and run.

Waking with a start, it took her a moment to realize that she'd been having a nightmare. Phew, that had felt so real. She smiled as she remembered the movie footage that they'd replayed earlier. It had been fun playing clueless twins with Jessie.

She glanced around the tent and saw three sleeping shapes. Someone was missing. Sassy. Maybe she'd got up to go to the loo? She checked her phone – 6.12 a.m.

After a few more minutes, Lucy carefully slid out of her sleeping bag, so as not to wake the others, and crept out of the tent. It was early morning and the ground was wet from rain. She vaguely remembered hearing thunder during the night. She put on her wellies and walked down to the toilet block, but Sassy wasn't there. Weird.

When she got back to the tent, she shook Abby awake. 'Do you know where Sassy's g-gone?' she whispered. 'Sh-she's not here.'

'Gone? What do you mean, gone?' asked Hermione, who had woken up too.

'Well, sh-she's not here or at the toilets. I checked,' Lucy replied. 'I walked around the campsite on the w-way back too.'

'Could she have gone down to the lake? Maybe she forgot something there last night?' suggested Abby.

'Dunno. Let's go see . . .' said Lucy, feeling a bit panicky. 'H, you s-stay here in case she comes back.'

Jessie was still fast asleep, so they didn't disturb her.

But there was no sign of Sassy when they got down to the dock. Lucy had run out of places to look.

'I think I've g-gotta tell my p-parents,' Lucy said, her voice wavering. 'I d-don't know what else to do.'

'What if something's happened to her or she's been kidnapped?' Abby asked dramatically.

'Shut up, Abs!' said Lucy, feeling really upset.

By the time they got back to the campsite, Lucy's parents were up and starting to make coffee. Maggie was jumping in puddles and greeted them enthusiastically when she spotted them. Lucy didn't know how to break the news.

'Morning, girls! You're up early,' said Lucy's dad.

'Dad, I'm really w-worried,' said Lucy, starting to cry. 'S-sassy's m-missing.'

'What? Missing? How?' he asked sharply.

Mrs Lockwood emerged quickly from their tent. 'Tell me,' she said, turning to Abby because Lucy was sobbing and couldn't speak.

'Sassy's not in the tent. We've also checked at the toilets and down by the lake – no sign of her,' Abby replied.

'Do you have any idea where she might have gone?' Mrs Lockwood asked.

Lucy shook her head miserably. 'What are we going to do?' she said to her husband.

'Why LucyLoo crying?' asked Maggie, frowning with concern.

'Don't worry, sweetie,' murmured her mother.

Lucy tried to smile reassuringly at her sister, but her heart was pounding.

'We'll have to do a thorough search of the entire campsite,' said Mr Lockwood, running his hand through his hair. 'Spread out, look everywhere and ask all the campers if they've seen her. We'll need to alert the camp officials to get some help. If that doesn't work, we'll need to inform the police . . .'

Lucy started crying again. She couldn't believe this was happening.

'Shall I call her dad now?' asked Lucy's mum.

'No, leave it for the moment,' replied Mr Lockwood. 'Let's do the search first. We'll need everyone to help.

What about those boys you've made friends with? Has anyone checked with them?'

Lucy couldn't believe she hadn't thought of that. 'I'm n-not sure where their t-tent is, but I'll ask the others.'

Back in the tent, Jessie said, 'Are you sure this isn't just a Sassy prank?'

They all looked shocked.

'I hope not,' said Hermione seriously.

'Look, her phone is here, but her vlog camera is missing,' observed Abby. 'Maybe she went off filming?'

Lucy felt a stab of hope. It would explain things . . . and Sassy had been keen to shoot some extra scenes last night. But why hadn't she left a note or something?

Mr Lockwood enlisted the help of the campsite officials. The girls went from family to family asking if anyone had seen the girl with the purple hair. But no luck, and the boys and their families hadn't heard from Sassy either.

An hour later, they regrouped at the Lockwoods' tent. Lucy could hear her mother on the phone to Sassy's father.

'I'm sure it will be all right,' reassured Mrs Lockwood. 'I'm sure – yes . . . yes . . . Well of course . . . yes . . . I understand if you want to come.'

He was obviously angry and upset.

'Luce, I think we may need to involve the police,' said Mr Lockwood grimly.

Lucy was so worried, she felt sick to her stomach, and even Abby had gone quiet.

Finn and Leo appeared. 'We've just come from the lake,' Finn said. 'The man in charge of the boats noticed there's a kayak missing. We're going out on the lake to help look for her, in case she went out in it.'

'That could be a hopeful sign,' said Lucy's mum encouragingly. 'Thanks, boys. Girls, why don't you take the binoculars and see if you can spot anything on the lake?'

Lucy's imagination soared. What if Sassy was at the bottom of the lake . . . ? Ghost Girl was no longer a laughing matter.

Down at the dock all the boats were deployed to search the lake, the far shore and the island. Jessie insisted on joining the search party, but Lucy, Hermione and Abby stayed on the shore.

'Would she have a-actually gone out in the b-boat on her own, at n-night?' asked Lucy. It seemed so unlikely – she didn't know Sassy all that well yet, but surely this was reckless behaviour by anyone's standards.

'Maybe,' replied Abby. 'I mean, she was pretty obsessed with this movie.'

'But it would have been crazy to go out on her own, especially in a storm,' observed Hermione.

Lucy secretly wished that Sassy hadn't come. Maybe she was just too wild and impulsive for them to keep up with her. But she kept her thoughts to herself.

*

The search party was gone for a couple of hours, by which time Mr Lockwood had called the police to send help and put Maggie in the crèche to avoid her cottoning on to what was happening and getting upset. Lucy and the others returned to the campsite. Eventually Finn came back to report that they'd found a paddle floating in a distant part of the lake.

'Is that . . . g-good?' asked Lucy, feeling too anxious to make sense of anything.

'I don't think so,' said Hermione, going green. 'I mean, what happened to the kayak? Did it capsize?'

Lucy started to cry again, and they all hugged each other.

This can't be happening, she thought. *It's a nightmare.*

'Girls, you must be starving. You didn't have any breakfast,' said her mother, also giving her a hug. She made them some sandwiches, which they ate despondently, in silence, and then went off with Lucys dad to speak to the police who had arrived.

Suddenly Jessie came running up from the lake.

'They've found her,' she shouted breathlessly, 'on the little island.'

'Is sh-she OK?' asked Lucy, her mouth going dry.

'Yup! She's alive and fine – well, unless she's got hypothermia. You won't believe this, but she spent the night on that island. She was drenched from the thunderstorm and freezing cold. She's wrapped in one of those silver blanket thingies,' said Jessie. 'You know the ones marathon runners get at the end of the race?' She bent over, breathing hard.

'It's to regulate body temperature,' explained Hermione. 'Astronauts use them too—'

'Who cares about astronauts! What on earth was Sassy doing on the island?' interrupted Abby. 'Let's go down to see her.'

'They're bringing her here,' said Jessie. 'Let's get a hot drink ready.'

Sassy looked exhausted and bedraggled when they were finally reunited. Her hair and clothes were wet, and she was shivering even under the thermal blanket.

Lucy anxiously thrust a mug of hot tea into her hand.

'First things first, Sassy. Call your dad and tell him you're safe. He's worried sick and is about to get in the car to come here,' said Mrs Lockwood, gently twisting Sassy's hair to wring out the water. 'Then let's get you into some dry clothes.'

'Tell us what happened!' clamoured Abby once Sassy had called her dad. 'And don't miss out a single detail!'

Finally the story came out. Sassy had gone down to the lake around midnight to film the lightning and storm. On the spur of the moment, she decided to go out on to the lake to get a full 360-degree shot, with the lightning flashes reflected in the water, so she took one of the boats. Then the lightning came very close and started to strike the water. She knew she was in danger of getting hit, so she started to paddle towards the island in a panic. Somehow she managed to drop the paddle in the water and it floated away. She tried to reach it but couldn't. (Lucy winced here, imagining how panicky she must have felt.) In desperation, Sassy paddled using just her hands until she reached the shore of the island . . .

'Then I collapsed with exhaustion and fell asleep!' she concluded. 'And woke up stranded. The rest you know.'

The girls stared at her, still drinking in the story. 'That was NOT cool to go down to the lake alone, Sass!' exclaimed Abby. 'But we're so hashtag *relieved* you're OK.'

'W-we thought m-maybe you'd d-drowned,' said Lucy quietly.

'No fear of that!' Sassy laughed. 'And I did get some great footage.'

Lucy felt herself choke up and grow angry. Didn't Sassy realize what she had put them through? Apart from frightening her friends, she had worried Lucy's parents, alarmed the entire campsite, and the police had been summoned! Sassy hadn't thought about anyone besides herself. It was all just about her film, her adventure. It was all about her.

Hermione grabbed Lucy's hand and led her away

from the others. 'I know what you're thinking, and I agree,' she said. 'It was totally selfish. She should at least apologize.'

Lucy nodded. 'Exactly, I know sh-she's had an awful time, but s-so have we.'

When the police had gone and everything was getting back to normal at the campsite, Lucy's dad finally asked, 'Sassy, what did you think you were doing? You were expressly forbidden from roaming the woods at night and on your own, and, furthermore, I specifically said no one was to go out on the lake at night. You broke every rule . . . Do you understand the trouble you've caused?'

'Your father was frantic with worry,' added Mrs Lockwood.

Lucy squirmed – it was weird watching her parents tell off one of her friends.

'I'm sorry,' replied Sassy sheepishly. 'I didn't mean to cause any trouble . . . I didn't think anyone would ever know I'd gone out for a bit . . . It seemed pretty harmless.

I didn't know I was going to drop that paddle—'

'That's not the point!' exploded Lucy's dad. 'You deliberately broke the rules. You're our guest; we're responsible for you when you're with us. You showed no concern for that . . .' He walked away. Lucy had rarely seen him so angry.

'Sassy, I'll be speaking to your father later,' said Lucy's mum gently. 'I'm not sure what he has planned for you, but I'm sure there will be consequences. He was extremely worried, and I doubt he'll allow you to stay on till the end of the week.'

Sassy apologized again, then walked off arm-in-arm with Abby, and Lucy crept into her parents' tent and lay down for a bit. She felt tired and drained. She was happy that Sassy was safe, of course, but the whole thing had been a horrible experience. She wished Sam were there to give her a cuddle. She'd try to ring him later, but she knew he was working at City Farm that morning.

*

Dinner was awkward: everyone quite formal and polite, with none of the usual chatter and joking. Lucy's parents said nothing until the end when Lucy's mum spoke.

'I've called your father, Sassy, and persuaded him to let you stay on.'

'Yay!' said Abby, and Sassy gave her a big smile.

Lucy didn't know what to think, or how to feel.

'Thank you, Mrs Lockwood,' Sassy said. 'I appreciate it and, once again, I'm really sorry for all the trouble I caused.'

'BUT,' Lucy's mum continued, 'Lucy's dad and I think that under the circumstances, considering the events of last night, the visit to Chesterbury Festival has to be cancelled. It doesn't seem appropriate.'

Later that night, Lucy pulled out her phone in the darkness of the tent.

23:04

Lucy: You there?

23:06

Sam: Hi! Everything OK? I miss you!

23:06

Lucy: WORST DISASTER OF MY LIFE!

23:06

Lucy: (I miss you too xxx)

23:07

Sam: ??? What happened?

23:09

Lucy: We just got GROUNDED!
Can't go to Chesterbury! Sooo unfair.

23:09

Sam: Why?

23:11

Lucy: Sassy snuck out. Got in BIG trouble. My parents flipped! Now they won't let any of us go! And Abby can't do the radio interview. Tiffany will hate us.

23:12

Sam: Brutal.

23:14

Lucy: I am so MAD! Will never forgive her for spoiling this!

23:14

Sam: Whoa! Never heard you so angry . . . try to relax.

23:14

Lucy: But I'm so upse

23:16

Sam: Maybe try to talk to your parents again?

23:17

Lucy: No point. They won't even let us vlog tonight . . . not that we feel like it anyway.

23:17

Sam: Don't feel like vlogging? Must be bad!

23:18

Lucy: Har har. Not funny!

23:18

Sam: Speaking of vlogs . . . been watching your old LucyLocket videos . . . you and Foghorn, pretty cute x

23:19

Lucy: OMG so embarrassing pls don't watch those!

23:20

Sam: Try and stop me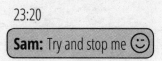

23:21

Lucy: Thought you hated YouTube haha. OK gotta go sleep. Miss you so much!!! xxxx

23:21

Sam: Keep me posted. BH. XXX

Lucy switched off her phone and snuggled down into her sleeping bag. Sam always made her feel better, but could things get any worse? None of the girls were really speaking to each other . . . How would they get through tomorrow?

Chapter Eight:
Hermione

Hermione woke early and crept out of the tent. She was going to offer to make sausage sandwiches for breakfast to cheer everyone up, but first she sat down at the picnic table to write in her diary.

Dear Diary,

Relieved I made room for you in my rucksack, even if I did have to sacrifice some comfy walking socks! I seriously need to offload. Yesterday was the most AWFUL day. Not the worst of my life, cos we all know that was when I found out my parents were splitting up, but this was up there in my top five!

First of all, there was the stress of Sassy going missing and the worry that she might actually have drowned. Lucy especially was SO upset. Then when she'd been found, Sassy didn't really see that what she'd done was wrong and inconsiderate. I mean, she seemed to think it was all a big joke. And finally there was the huge disappointment when we were banned from going to Chesterbury. We had just agreed to interview some festival-goers about their outfits for a local radio station. Tiffany arranged it for us. How cool would that have been? Abby would probably have done the interviewing, but we were all excited for the publicity it would give GCV, so now we're missing out on that as well as the fun of being at a festival. And Abby doesn't get to see Charlie.

Long story short, we're all completely gutted, but because Sassy is here we haven't been able to express our feelings to each other. I can tell everyone is furious with her for spoiling everything, even Abby, who usually thinks she walks on water. We've still got three days left of the trip, and I don't know how it's going to play out. And, as for Leo, I bumped into him just now as he was heading off to the showers. He looked all cute and half asleep still. We haven't spent any proper time together, but I really—

'Oh, Hermione, you're up,' said Mrs Lockwood, crawling out of her tent. 'Hard at work on one of your stories?'

'Yes, Mrs Lockwood. Well, kind of,' said Hermione, slamming her diary shut. 'Need a hand with breakfast?'

Breakfast was quiet, and Hermione thought everyone looked rather grumpy: heads down and eyes heavy as if they hadn't got much sleep. Hermione certainly hadn't. She couldn't stop thinking about what they were going to do about Sassy.

'I'm sensing that we need to blow some cobwebs away,' said Mr Lockwood through a mouthful of sausage, 'so we're going on the 10k hike up to the Devil's Tor. I hope everyone's ready for that. You'll need your hiking boots and a rain jacket, just in case, as well as sandwiches and plenty of water. Put some sunscreen on too – we might get lucky!'

Sounds exhausting, thought Hermione. Ten kilometres was a looooong way. She'd much prefer to stay cosied up with her book. Or hang around the campsite in the hope of seeing Leo again.

'We going to see the devil?' asked Maggie, looking worried.

Her father laughed and kissed her on top of the head. 'No, sweetpea. Just for a lovely long walk.'

Mr Lockwood sounded much cheerier than yesterday, but as Hermione scanned the faces of her friends, she could see little enthusiasm. Sassy's expression was hard to pinpoint – a mixture of defiance and anxiety.

They reached the beginning of the trail and headed off up the track. Jessie, Abby and Lucy forged ahead, leaving Hermione and Sassy to walk together.

Hermione wasn't exactly thrilled to be walking with Sassy, but she couldn't abandon her and join the others – the path wasn't wide enough, for one thing, plus it would seem kind of mean. She knew what it was like to be on the outside. But, still, this was going to be mega awkward.

'I'm not sure these Converse are the best

shoes for hiking, but I don't actually have hiking
boots,' Sassy said, looking down at her purple
All Stars.

'Well, I've got some plasters and stuff, if you
need them later,' offered Hermione grudgingly.

They hiked in silence until, after about fifteen minutes,
Sassy finally spoke. 'So, I get that everyone is pretty
angry with me. I mean I've spoilt everyone's big treat of
the summer – haven't I?' She glanced at Hermione.

Hermione was silent for a bit – she didn't know quite
how to answer – but then she drew a deep breath and
jumped right in. 'Well, yeah, we are disappointed to be
missing out on Chesterbury. And it does seem unfair
that everyone's being punished . . . It's like at school when
the whole class gets detention because one person has
done something wrong. Kind of harsh.'

'I get that,' said Sassy. 'Believe me, I didn't mean to
cause any trouble with the search party and the police
and all that. When I realized how angry the Lockwoods
were, I expected I would be punished, but not the rest

of you. I just thought they'd send me home.'

'So did I,' admitted Hermione. 'Also I thought that, if they didn't, your dad would send for you. He seems kind of . . . protective.'

Sassy rolled her eyes. 'You can say that again. It's a miracle he let me stay. Anyway –' she glanced miserably ahead at the three girls in front of them, who hadn't looked back once – 'everyone is going to hate me forever, right? I guess I'm going to have to quit the channel.'

'I wouldn't say that,' Hermione said, suddenly feeling sorry for Sassy. 'You've only just joined! But no one knows that you're sorry. Everyone got the impression that you just thought this was a big joke. I think they're angrier at you for your attitude than anything else.'

'Really?' Sassy looked thoughtful. 'Well, sometimes when I don't know how to act, I get a bit obnoxious, maybe? I pretend I don't care about anything. I don't mean to, but it comes out that way.'

'I understand,' said Hermione. She knew loads of people who sometimes acted like that, including Abby.

'But the big question is, what are you going to do to make this better?'

They reached the top of the tor by lunchtime and had a picnic by the big rock. There had been quite a lot of moaning for the last steep climb (especially from Maggie, who had to be bribed with sweets to keep going) and Hermione was limping due to a large blister.

The view looked amazing, and Hermione took lots of photos and panning shots over the valley. You could see the ocean far away in the distance.

After lunch, during which all the girls, apart from Hermione, were still quite frosty to Sassy, Sassy drew Mrs Lockwood aside, and they went off for a walk along the ridge while the others lay sunbathing. They were gone for ages.

'What d'you reckon they're talking about?' asked Jessie lazily.

'Dunno,' said Hermione. 'I think Sassy's feeling a bit down.'

'Abs, d-did you hear back from T-Tiffany about how we won't be coming?' asked Lucy.

'Yeah, she's really disappointed. Though not as much as I am,' replied Abby with a sigh. 'I was so ready to try out my festival look.'

'I know,' said Lucy sadly. 'I'm s-sorry the trip has turned out this way.'

'It's not your fault,' replied Abby, twirling a daisy between her fingers. 'I don't know how I could've been so wrong about Sassy. I guess I sort of got dazzled by her energy and didn't see how selfish she is.'

'Well, maybe she just comes across that way because she's feeling insecure,' said Hermione tentatively. She wasn't completely sure why she was defending Sassy, but it felt like the right thing to do.

Jessie nodded. 'Could be. Well, I'm just relieved I'm off the hook,' she joked.

Abby tutted. 'Please stop going on about that, Jess. It's old news! The problem with Sassy is that she needs all this attention—'

'Shh, they're c-coming back,' warned Lucy, and that was the end of the discussion.

The way down was easier than the way up, although Maggie protested and had to be carried on Mr Lockwood's shoulders.

'Shall we have ice cream when we get back down? There's meant to be a great place nearby. It's all homemade,' said Mrs Lockwood.

The girls nodded eagerly.

The rows of brightly coloured ice cream looked amazing, and Hermione took some pictures for her Instagram. There were thirty flavours and loads of toppings you could get sprinkled over. They took ages to make their choices: Lucy had vanilla and chocolate chip with salted caramel sauce; Abby chose rocky road with gummy bears; Jessie went for peanut butter with fudge pieces; Sassy chose mango with raspberry sauce; and, after much deliberation, Hermione picked coconut with nuts on top.

They sat outside at a picnic table, licking and slurping, while Lucy's parents sat a little distance away with Maggie, deep in conversation.

'Wow, I needed that sugar hit,' said Sassy.

There was a pause.

Then: 'Me too,' agreed Hermione. They couldn't freeze Sassy out forever.

After a few seconds Abby joined in. 'Totally. Gummy bears as an ice-cream topping – mind blown!'

They all began to chat enthusiastically about the best flavour combinations, and there seemed to be an unspoken agreement to move on from what had happened.

By the time they got back to the campsite, Hermione had something else on her mind. On the way to the showers that morning, Leo had told her that he and his friends were leaving tomorrow. Now she was dying to see him one last time before he left. They hadn't spent much time together, but she really liked him – he made her laugh and knew loads of fascinating, random facts. She felt as if she could spend hours in his company and never get bored.

But did he like her? She thought maybe he did, but it was so hard to tell with boys . . . and she'd been wrong before. Would Leo want to stay in touch? It was so nerve-wracking.

'Luce, come for a walk with me?' she asked as the others went to change in the tent. 'I was thinking we could go down to the lake.'

'M-more walking?' groaned Lucy. 'What about your b-blisters?'

'They feel better,' said Hermione quickly. Which was not true – she was actually in mild agony. 'We don't have to go for long,' she added pleadingly.

Lucy laughed. 'I know who you're l-looking for . . .' she teased affectionately. 'He s-seems so nice, and I think he likes you.'

Hermione blushed. 'D'you think so?' she asked. 'I can never tell. But he does make me laugh. And he's Ravenclaw too.'

*

There were lots of people milling round the dock. Hermione's heart leaped as she caught sight of Leo and his friends.

'OMG, he's c-coming over,' said Lucy excitedly. 'Like a moth to a f-flame!'

'Shut up,' giggled Hermione, swishing her hair out of her face. She panicked as Lucy walked off and pretended to make a phone call, leaving the two of them alone.

'Hey,' said Leo, giving her a little wave.

'Hey,' she replied. There was a long silence. Finally she said, 'You OK?'

'Yeah, we're just having our last sesh on the lake before packing up. Do you . . . do you wanna come out in the kayak with me?' Leo asked. 'I could do with the help – my arms are knackered!'

'Erm, OK,' replied Hermione.

She gestured to Lucy to explain what was happening, then they put on some life jackets and got in the boat, Hermione praying that she wouldn't do an Abby and fall out. She managed to get in safely, then sat in front, which was a bit awkward because it meant she couldn't see Leo's face. They paddled on in silence for a bit.

'It's sort of like the Great Lake, isn't it?' Hermione blurted, feeling her face flush.

'You think?' She could hear him smiling.

'This is how I picture it anyway, all peaceful—'

A child screamed with laughter somewhere over by the inflatables.

'OK, without the inflatables and with a giant squid, but you know what I mean.'

'Where is there a giant squid in *Harry Potter*?'

Hermione sighed. 'This is what happens when you don't read the books, Leo. You miss things.'

He laughed. 'I promise I'll at least start reading the books before I see you next. How about that?'

Hermione nearly dropped her paddle. 'When you see me next?'

'Well, I was thinking, maybe we can meet up later in

the summer . . .' said Leo hesitantly.

Hermione grinned, safe in the knowledge that he couldn't see her. *Yessss!*

'I mean if you're up for it, and not too busy? I think we're only a couple of hours' drive away.'

She savoured the moment for a couple of seconds. 'That'd be great,' she said casually. 'I'm going away with my dad at the end of the summer, but otherwise I'm around.'

'Might be cool to do the *Harry Potter* movie challenge together,' said Leo. 'Have you ever done it?'

'Not the whole thing. I read it takes nineteen hours and thirty-nine minutes to watch all eight movies back to back! Maybe you could come to my house? I'd have to ask my mum if you could stay over, but I think it'd be OK.' It would definitely not be OK with her mum, but Hermione could cross that bridge when she came to it.

'Nice one,' said Leo.

She summoned up her courage and turned round to give him a little smile, which he returned. She turned back and grinned to herself again.

He likes me, he likes me!

When they got back to the dock and out of the kayak, it was a little strange, not least because Lucy was watching them from a few metres away.

Leo said, 'OK, gotta go, Hermione. I'll text you when I get home. Be good!'

'Ha – you too!' replied Hermione, heart racing as Leo leaned forward and gave her a quick hug.

They exchanged numbers and promised to look each other up on Facebook.

'Don't forget to wear suncream!' she called after him, giggling, as he walked away.

Hermione felt herself glow with a warm feeling as she and Lucy walked back to the campsite. She was glad Lucy didn't ask too many questions; she was blissfully lost in her thoughts.

Dinner was hamburgers and hotdogs, the best meal they'd had so far. The girls quizzed Hermione about her romantic kayak trip until Mrs Lockwood cut in.

'Leave the poor girl alone!' she said with a smile, which Hermione returned gratefully. 'Besides, I have something to tell all of you. I had a long talk today with Sassy. She wanted to explain what really happened yesterday. She apologized once again for causing such an uproar and, more importantly, she offered to go home so that you four could go to Chesterbury. She felt it was unfair that you should be punished for something that wasn't your fault.'

They all looked at Sassy, who shrugged. 'It's true.'

'So I've been discussing the situation with Lucy's dad, and we've decided to let you go to Chesterbury after all,' finished Mrs Lockwood.

'Yay!' shouted Abby, before quickly slapping her hand over her mouth. 'Sorry.'

They girls looked more stunned than happy, but slowly smiles crept back on to their faces.

Hermione reached over and squeezed Sassy's hand. 'Well done!' she said.

'Oh, Mom, thank you, thank you,' said Lucy, and

rushed over to give her mother a big hug. 'But what about S-Sassy? She can't stay h-here alone.'

'She's coming too,' said Lucy's mum. 'We decided she'd been punished enough. So you'd better get your outfits ready for tomorrow and get a good night's sleep. We're going to have a very early start, as we need to make two trips to get us all there!'

'Oh – and Sassy – no sneaking out on to the lake,' said Mr Lockwood.

'NOT FUNNY!' cried Sassy, as they all dissolved into laughter.

Dear Diary,

Woohoo! Chesterbury is back on! And Leo wants to come visit. I promise to record it all in your beautiful pages, diary of mine, so get ready!

Love,
Hermione

VLOG 7

Festival Make-up and Hair
12:22

FADE IN: ABBY and SASSY in service station loos, filming in front of basin and mirror. There are people walking in and out of shot, some looking sheepishly at the camera.

ABBY

So today is my final festival make-up vlog. I've really enjoyed your comments and suggestions on the earlier ones. I'm going to be giving Sassy a knock-out makeover to get her ready . . . as we are FINALLY on our way to Chesterbury!

ABBY gestures around.

ABBY (CONTINUED)

As you can see it's not the most glamorous of locations, but we don't have time to do this at the festival. You ready, Sass?

SASSY

So ready! It's been nearly a week since I did my make-up. I can't wait to see what you're gonna do.

ABBY

(to camera)

Unfortunately we don't have as much stuff as if we were in my bedroom, but we're gonna have to manage. By the way, the people here think we are crazy, ha ha!

ABBY waves at a middle-aged woman staring at them as she washes and dries her hands.

ABBY

Anyway, I've got all the important bits here with me, and I've found this little stool for Sassy to sit on, so let's get started! We

have to be quick cos Lucy's dad is waiting to drive us once we've finished filming. So today I'm going for a silvery-blue look to tie in with Sassy's purple hair and her mermaidy outfit. Trust me when I say we are pulling out ALL the stops.

SASSY

Yesss!

ABBY

So, first of all, apply moisturizer all over your face, or you could use a primer.

ABBY squeezes moisturizer out of a tube and puts it on Sassy.

ABBY (CONTINUED)

Then put concealer round your eyes and apply foundation with
a brush. Blend it all in nicely. Next I'm using some highlighter
on your cheekbones.

ABBY dots it on.

ABBY (CONTINUED)

I got this really cool iridescent rainbow highlighter especially
for our festival make-up. I can't wait to use it myself!

SASSY turns her head to catch the light.

SASSY

Wow, that looks amazing.
You are such a pro!

ABBY

Ha ha, I wish! Now the eyes. First
a silver eyeshadow cream on your lids, but also down under

your eyes. Then, on top of that, I'm applying some of this turquoise eyeshadow. Then a thick black eyeliner with a feline flick to make your eyes really striking.

ABBY concentrates hard on applying the eyeliner, her tongue poking out of her mouth.

ABBY (CONTINUED)

Nice! Now black mascara followed by bright blue mascara on your top lashes, and finally I'm putting the silver eyeshadow on your bottom lashes, followed by the blue mascara.

ABBY hums as she does this.

ABBY (CONTINUED)

Then we'll do the brows very thickly so they look really dramatic, and finish by brushing some blue mascara on the brows too.

SASSY

Wow, my eyes look insane!

LUCY appears behind them in shot.

LUCY

How much longer? Dad's g-getting restless.

(pause)

Wow, S-Sassy, you look INCREDIBLE!

SASSY

Thanks, Luce.

ABBY

Ten minutes, we're hurrying!

(pause)

Next, I've got these strips of stick-on jewels that I'm gonna apply above Sassy's brows and in the centre of her forehead. You can use these straight out of a packet; it isn't difficult to do. You can even add some extra drama by applying some dots with this black liquid eyeliner or tattoo liner.

ABBY applies jewels.

ABBY
Doesn't that look great?

SASSY
Very Bollywood!

ABBY
I know! Now for some glitter. First I apply Vaseline to make the glitter stick, here under the eyes. Dab it on lightly and then using your finger just dab the glitter on top in half circles under your eyes and on to your cheekbones. I'm using silver holographic glitter.

SASSY
This was made for me.

ABBY

And to finish, we now need to do the lips. I'm gonna use this blue liquid suede cream lipstick, which gives a really vibrant colour. Not my usual colour, it was in a pack of three, and I haven't used it yet. But if anyone can rock it, SassySays can!

ABBY paints on the lipstick.

ABBY

Ooh, it's so bright.

SASSY

Love it! Can I keep it?

ABBY

It's all yours!

SASSY

Yesss, thank you! And now what are we doing for hair?

ABBY

That's easy. Your hair already has these great blue streaks. I'm going to make two ponytails on top of your head and then wrap them round to make space buns and pin them in place.

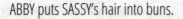

ABBY puts SASSY's hair into buns.

ABBY

Sorry – I kind of rushed that, but don't they look cute?

SASSY

Yeah, they remind me of Princess Leia. Nice!

ABBY

Now I'm adding some glitter to your hair parting. Also some

hair chalk just to jazz up the colour of your hair. I think I'll add some green for the mermaidy look. And finally I'm going to make a couple of skinny plaits and add some silver beads for some extra texture.

ABBY takes in SASSY's whole look.

ABBY (CONTINUED)

Wow! You look incredible, if I say so myself.

SASSY

There's only one word for it: SLAY!

ABBY

(to camera)

So I hope that gives you guys some ideas for how to do your make-up for going to a festival or a fancy-dress party. It's not as hard as you think, so give it a go! If you'd like me to do some more special-occasion make-up looks, let me know in the comments down below. I'm also adding links to all the products I used. Thanks for watching. I need to run and grab

a takeaway coffee before Lucy's dad drives off without us.

Bye-ee!

SASSY

Byee!!

In the background we can hear different voices. 'Look at that

girl, she's got blue lipstick on!' 'It takes all sorts . . .' 'Must be off

to Chesterbury . . .' 'Is she meant to be an alien?'

Views: 21,732

Subscribers: 27,385

Comments:

xxrainbowxx: Beautifullll 😍

StephSaysHi: 😃 That woman walking into shot at 2:09!

hamiltonlife: hair goals . . . NEED that glitter!

ShyGirl1: I would be scared to wear that colour lipstick but it's sooo cool!

livvydoesmakeup: I post make-up tutorials too plz check
out my channel ♥

MagicMorgan: SLAY indeed!

(scroll down to see 19 more comments)

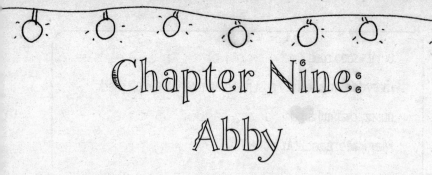

Chapter Nine:
Abby

'OMG, I can't believe how GINORMOUS this place is,' exclaimed Abby as they entered the festival, having got their wristbands, site maps and programmes. They agreed a meeting time and place, promised to stick together, and then Lucy's dad headed off. The girls were on their own.

Abby looked around, drinking it all in. Before her, as far as the eye could see, was a riot of colour, flags, bunting, fairy lights, a ribbon tower, a helter-skelter, sand sculptures, gigantic robotic spiders and what seemed like millions of stalls and food trucks. In the distance she could see the sound stages for the bands, and the surrounding hills were covered with tents and teepees right up to a huge sign that said CHESTERBURY in multicoloured lights.

'I never imagined it would be this big,' said Jessie in awe.

'Just look at all the people,' added Hermione.

Noticing some nice outfits, Abby was reminded of their radio gig, and she snapped into GCV manager mode. 'We better get over to the VIP area and try to meet up with Tiffany. I've got our passes to the hospitality area. I think it's over there.'

'Does Tiffany know we are c-coming?' asked Lucy.

'Yeah, I texted her and Charlie last night, but she didn't reply. Anyway, let's hurry up.'

It was hard to stay focused on walking straight ahead as the stalls on either side of the path were filled with tempting things to buy: cool clothes, sparkly accessories, lots of jewellery and hair and body decorations. It was like a giant Claire's—

Abby's phone beeped.

11:45

Charlie: Are you here yet?

11:45

Abby: Yup. On way to VIP hospitality . . . come and meet us!

11:46

Charlie: I'm here waiting! But hurry – Dakota is here too, ready to take your place! xx PS Can't wait to see you x

11:47

Abby: Nooooo stop her! We're coming!

11:48

Abby: Can't wait to see you too xxx

'Guys, we've got to hurry. Dakota's taking over,' Abby snapped, doubling her speed. 'I told Tiffany we were back on. Why aren't they waiting?'

They reached the VIP area, showed their passes, got their VIP wristbands and entered a large open hospitality area surrounded by fancy-looking tents. It was a lot less crowded in here. People in expensive-looking wellies were chilling out on sofas and deck chairs and sipping cocktails. A few people were dancing to some weird music. Someone was getting a massage on a massage table. There were delicious smells of cooking and lots of food stalls. In the tents was a pamper parlour and a nail art and henna tattoo place as well as a photo booth.

'Wow!' said Jessie. 'So this is what it's like to be a celeb! It's so cool.'

'Abby! Abby!' Abby turned as Charlie ran up to her and gave her a big hug.

'Oh, it's good to see you, babe!' said Abby, hugging him back. She'd missed him more than she'd realized.

'Hey there! It's the whole squad!' he said, greeting the others. 'So Dakota is here and says she's doing the live radio feed for Radio Fresh. I told her you were on your way, but she wouldn't listen. She's over there with the mic.'

'Oh no!' cried Lucy, looking over. 'We were

m-meant to be d-doing that!'

'Don't worry, we will!' insisted Abby. 'But where's Tiffany? She's the one who set this up.'

'I can't see her. She was here earlier, but maybe she's had to go do something else,' said Charlie.

Then Abby spotted Dakota: she looked amazing. She was wearing a green sequinned mermaid playsuit with a spangled shirt over the top of it, a headdress with pompom earrings, and her face was bejewelled with the gems that Abby had shown on a previous vlog back home. In fact, her make-up was a complete copy of that tutorial . . .

'I just found these ah-mazing unicorn gems online,' Dakota was telling someone. 'Nobody was wearing them yet. And then I decided to do this glitter thing under the eyes—'

Abby saw red. How dare Dakota take credit for her look and ideas? She wouldn't stand for this! She marched over towards Dakota with the girls following behind her.

'Oi!' she shouted. 'You copycat! You wannabe!'

Dakota turned and looked at her with disgust. 'What are you losers doing here? Don't you know you've been replaced? Tiffany needed someone she could rely on – like moi!'

Abby's fury hit the next level and she snatched the mic out of Dakota's hand. The radio sound crew stood frozen with horror. They couldn't understand what was happening.

'Tiffany will sort this out,' said Jessie to the others. 'I'll go and look for her.' She hurried off.

Dakota lunged towards Abby and grabbed the mic, but Abby didn't let go. They started to tug it back and forth. A small crowd was gathering around them.

'You go, girls!' someone shouted, and the crowd laughed.

'This is t-terrible,' moaned Lucy. 'Charlie, we have to st-stop this.'

Charlie moved forward to try to intervene, and Dakota gave him a big shove. When Abby saw this, she

leaned right into Dakota's face and shouted,
'You are fake news!'

Dakota was so taken aback that she let go of the mic.

'Hey, hey, ladies. Let's all chill!' Tiffany said, arriving on the scene and sounding a bit annoyed.

Both Abby and Dakota stepped back, and Abby felt a rush of embarrassment. It had been a few weeks since she'd seen the YouTube superstar, better known as RedVelvet, and Abby was mortified that she was seeing her at her worst.

'Abby, I'm so pleased you and the other GCV guys are here. I didn't think you were coming, which is why I accepted Dakota's offer to step in,' said Tiffany, who looked gorgeous in a tasselled white shirt over denim shorts and red leather cowboy boots.

'I texted you . . .' said Abby desperately. 'Maybe the reception was dodgy?'

'Oh, OK, well, no problem; I think we can use both of you.' She raised an eyebrow. 'IF we can keep it professional.'

'Of course,' said Abby, feeling she couldn't object, but not happy about Dakota being involved.

After a few minutes' briefing, Abby headed off with the sound crew to interview the festival-goers. In the meantime, Hermione had come up with an idea for the channel – so Sassy and Jessie went to help film that while Abby did the interviews, with Lucy by her side for back-up.

Abby spoke confidently into the mic. 'Some people think it's naff to dress up for festivals and that you should just wear jeans and wellies, but personally I love the idea of people expressing themselves with an amazing outfit. Like this lady! Excuse me, what's inspired your look today?' she asked a dark-haired girl wearing a flower crown, a brightly coloured peasant dress and silver jewellery.

'Well, I'm channelling Frida Kahlo – even the eyebrows!' She laughed, and pointed to her dark monobrow. 'Such a talented artist.'

'Fabulous!' said Abby, glossing over the fact that

she had no idea who Frida whatever was.

Lucy patted her on the arm and pointed at a young guy dressed in a silver jumpsuit with a unicorn horn and rainbow mane.

Abby hurried over, described his outfit for the radio listeners and then asked, 'What would you say you represent?'

'I'm the unicorn emoji – can't you tell?' he replied.

'Of course! I love it!' She giggled.

As Abby walked on, she observed, 'So, obviously, I'm seeing lots of glitter and stick-on jewels everywhere. Also some amazing henna tattoos. Lots of psychedelic headbands and tie-dye for that classic hippy look. I've also seen quite a few girls with their hair up in glittery Princess Leia buns, like my friend Sassy.'

She glanced at the sound crew, one of whom gave her a thumbs-up and mouthed. 'You're doing great.' Her confidence soaring, she continued. This felt so natural!

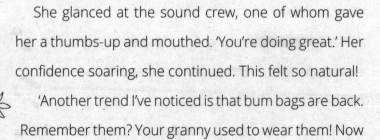

'Another trend I've noticed is that bum bags are back. Remember them? Your granny used to wear them! Now

I see them everywhere – neon pink with sequins, sleek leather, iridescent metallic ones. And super practical for festivals, of course.

'Excuse me, may I ask what you've got in your bum bag?' she asked a passing girl.

'It's for the r-radio,' explained Lucy in a whisper.

'Sure,' said the girl. 'My phone – of course – and a back-up battery. Some money. My concealer and lipgloss. Let me see . . . my hand sanitizer, some plasters in case I get blisters, and I've even managed to squeeze in some loo roll!'

'Essential!' Abby laughed.

They walked on.

'Trendy wellies are standard wear at festivals, and although it's not raining – at least not yet – they are still to be seen. My fave footwear today, though, are these rainbow Doc Martens worn here by . . .' She held the mic out.

'Chloe.'

'Chloe, tell me about the rest of your outfit,' said Abby.

'I'm wearing this simple floral dress, but I'm contrasting it with this camo army jacket to grunge it up a bit. And a fedora hat.'

'You look fantastic. Very Coachella!' said Abby.

She looked around for the next interviewee, but nobody stood out. Lucy pointed at Abby. Abby took a second to realize what she was getting at and then the penny dropped.

'Oh yeah! And, finally, my own outfit for today is this sequinned turquoise unitard, white trainers with pastel rainbow stripes, and a stick-on gem choker round my neck. I've also got a fringed statement jacket for when it gets colder later. It was sooo difficult to choose, but the most important thing about dressing for festivals is to wear what you feel comfortable in. This was Abby Pinkerton of the Girls Can Vlog channel reporting to you from Chesterbury. Be happy, guys!'

'Terrific,' said the radio producer, as Lucy silently applauded. 'We're going to take a short break now. See you later.'

Abby and Lucy walked out of the VIP hospitality area and into the festival crowds.

'You were a-amazing, Abs,' said Lucy. 'I d-don't know how you d-do it.'

'With loads of help from you!' said Abby, grateful for Lucy's support and encouragement. 'Anyway, I'm sure you could do it too. But, Luce, I am DESPERATE for the loo. Can you see one?'

They saw a long queue snaking outside a row of wooden huts.

'Yikes,' said Lucy,' I d-don't think these are as nice as the ones in the VIP z-zone.'

'Yuck, I know . . . but it will have to do,' Abby said, holding her breath. 'Euch! It absolutely stinks!' she said when she was next in line outside the toilet. 'I should've brought some perfume to spray.' When she finally opened the door, she shrieked, 'OMG. It's just a hole dropping to the ground! Luce! Help me!'

'Maybe the unitard wasn't such a g-good idea . . . p-practically speaking,' observed Lucy after they had emerged a few minutes later.

'No, I'll mention that in my next festival fashion tips,' conceded Abby sheepishly.

They'd agreed to meet Charlie over by the food trucks in the hospitality area where Prankingstein were going to film an ice-cream eating challenge. Josh was there waiting.

'Hey, sis!' he waved. 'How was camping? Bears didn't get ya?'

'Ha, ha, you idiot!' Abby replied, and gave her brother a friendly punch on the arm.

'What are you wearing? You look like a peacock!' He laughed.

'A gorgeous peacock,' said Charlie, arriving and giving Abby a kiss. 'OK, we need to get this challenge off the ground.'

A small crowd of Prankingstein fans had gathered and were waiting for them to start. Abby watched with bated breath. She loved watching the guys film. They had so much energy.

'So hi, guys!' began Charlie once they'd set up their cameras and lights. 'Welcome to Prankingstein at Chesterbury. Today's challenge is to eat ten ice-cream cones in the shortest time.'

'Before they melt!' added Josh. 'And to make this EXTRA exciting, we'd like to invite a couple of people from the crowd to join us in the challenge. Any volunteers?'

'Not her!' yelped Abby, catching sight of Dakota. Honestly, the girl was like a bad penny, always turning up where she wasn't wanted.

Dakota sneered at Abby. 'I couldn't possibly submit my body to such a punishment,' she drawled. 'My body is a temple.'

'Looks more like a ruin to me,' sniped Abby.

'Abs!' Lucy giggled, but Abby shrugged. If Dakota dished it out, she had to be able to take it too.

Two volunteers stepped forward from the crowd to join Prankingstein. One of them was a very pretty

redhead who giggled a lot, Abby noticed.

Each contestant was brought a tray with ten ice creams, and then they were off! There was now quite a crowd watching and cheering them on as they stuffed the ice cream into their mouths as fast as they could. Soon the ice cream was melting, and their faces were covered in gunk. They looked a mess – even the redhead, Abby noted with satisfaction.

'Argh! Brain freeze!' shouted Charlie, and stopped to rub his temples. 'I have to take a break.'

'Come on, Charlie,' Abby yelled. 'You can do this!' But he gave her an apologetic look as he shook his head.

'Loser!' shouted Josh, who was on his seventh cone and still going strong.

'Are you OK?' the pretty redhead asked Charlie in a concerned voice. She stretched her hand out to stroke his head. 'I can't eat any more, either.'

Abby bristled, but Charlie responded by stuffing another cone into his mouth.

The crowd did a countdown as Josh managed to

ram the last ice-cream cone into his mouth. Everyone cheered.

'I love ice cream, but that was d-disgusting!' Lucy laughed.

When the redhead pulled out a napkin and started to wipe Charlie's mouth, Abby couldn't stand it any longer. She lunged forward and snatched the napkin out of the girl's hand.

'Excuse me!' she said, leaning over to give Charlie a kiss on the mouth.

'Sor-ree!' said the girl, taken aback.

'Hungry are you?' Charlie laughed, and gave Abby another kiss.

Later Abby and Charlie wandered around the festival, holding hands.

'I really missed you,' said Charlie, 'but it sounds like you had a super-cool time with the SUPing and everything.'

'It was fun but a bit stressful to be honest,' confessed Abby. 'The whole Sassy episode was kind of a nightmare and made me realize a few things.' She sighed. 'I thought she was so perfect, and I kept putting her before the others, but maybe I got a little carried away.'

'How?' asked Charlie.

'Well, maybe I forgot how the strength of GCV is the mix of personalities and our chemistry. And sometimes I think I can come across a bit harsh . . . even if I don't mean it,' Abby said, thinking of Jessie.

'It's not too late to fix any of that,' observed Charlie, 'and the girls know you have a heart of gold in there somewhere.'

'I do?' Abby giggled.

'Well, if the rumours are true,' said Charlie with a grin. 'Now let's go and find the others and see how Hermione got on with her vlog.'

VLOG 8

FADE IN: CHESTERBURY MUSIC FESTIVAL.

HERMIONE standing with the main Chesterbury stage in the background.

HERMIONE

Hi, guys! So, as you know, we're in Chesterbury, and we're

having the BEST time. I've been people-watching and it's dawned on me how many different kinds of people come to festivals. So today I'm going to do a VIP versus Slumming It take on the festival experience.

HERMIONE looks a bit anxious.

HERMIONE (CONTINUED)

This is meant to be a funny vlog, so everything is more exaggerated than in real life. If it's not funny, then that's just . . . awkward.

(sighs)

As you guys know, this kind of video isn't really my area of expertise, but there aren't many books or cupcake recipes around here so I figured I'd try something new! Anyway, here goes! Let's begin with how you get to the festival.

HERMIONE wearing sunglasses and looking FAB-U-LOUS,

sashays down some steps looking very sophisticated.

HERMIONE (CONTINUED)

Hello, darlings! I'm relieved to be here at last. We had a
tedious delay at the heliport, and then the pilot had trouble
finding a place to land. There were hippies camped out all over
the landing field . . . so inconsiderate!

HERMIONE looking fed up, sitting in a car, hanging out of the
window.

HERMIONE (CONTINUED)

OMG. How much longer can this drive take? We've been in
a traffic jam for three hours, and we haven't even reached
Chesterbury. Traffic is at a standstill! We might have to get out
and walk the rest of the way.

(off camera)

Once you reach the festival you need to sort out your accommodation . . .

HERMIONE wearing sunglasses, outside a huge VIP yurt.

HERMIONE (CONTINUED)

Oh, darlings, I suppose I can agree to sleep in this air-conditioned luxury yurt, just for a few nights. Its bathroom is stuffed with luxurious shampoos and bath oils at least, and there's a rather good sound system. There's the hot tub  too, of course, a  fully stocked mini bar and even butler service, like at home!

HERMIONE standing next to a tiny tent.

HERMIONE (CONTINUED)

We've just trudged a mile to the campsite that's the furthest

from the main action, carrying all our gear. I'm exhausted!

We've pitched our tent on a slope as there was no other

available space. So I hope it doesn't rain and cause a

mudslide! No showers or toilets here, by the way, so I hope

everyone brought some deodorant!

(off camera)

Now it's time for lunch . . .

HERMIONE wearing sunglasses, fanning herself.

HERMIONE (CONTINUED)

There's a most fabulous choice of food available and of course one doesn't pay for it. There is everything from seafood to stirfries to curries, all made to order by a top chef. There are special vegetarian and vegan options too. Something to tempt everyone. For dessert I see some homemade cookies and brownies, fresh from the oven, and a wonderful selection of ice cream. To drink there are some rather good smoothies and juices made to order. I've asked for fresh mango with ginger as a pick-me-up. My butler is bringing it over when it's ready. Cheers!

HERMIONE (CONTINUED)

(miserably)

So I've been waiting in this line for almost an hour to get a hamburger, and then I'll have to queue up somewhere else to get a drink, by which time my hamburger will be cold! And it's all going to cost a fortune and I'll have to eat it standing up as there's nowhere to sit down. Then I'll spend the next twenty-four hours praying that it was cooked properly and I'm not going to come down with food poisoning.

(off camera)

And the biggest festival issue of them all . . . What about when you need a 'comfort break'?

HERMIONE wearing sunglasses.

HERMIONE (CONTINUED)

I'll just pop into this luxury Portaloo. It's spacious and the door locks. It's scented with Chanel No. 5 and has an admirable range of hand lotions to apply after you've washed your hands. And a mirror so I can touch up my expensive Dior make-up.

SLUMMING IT

HERMIONE (CONTINUED)

I've been queuing up for ages and I almost wet myself, but finally it's my turn. Eeew! Practically retching here. The pong is horrendous, the stalls are disgusting – I won't even try to describe them – and there is NO loo paper! Needless to say, there's nowhere to wash your hands. Lucky I brought some hand sanitizer!

CUT TO: HERMIONE standing outside the main entrance.

HERMIONE (CONTINUED)

OK, so that was just a taste of the real experience of attending a pop festival – from one extreme to another. Hope it made you laugh! Thanks to RedVelvet for allowing us access to the VIP area, even if we didn't actually get to stay in a yurt. Give us a thumbs-up below if you enjoyed this video.

FADE OUT.

Views: 15,416

Subscribers: 29,442

Comments:

PrankingsteinJosh: absolute lolz!

pink_sparkles: Cold burger in the rain . . . we've all been there ☹

violets_space: I would never go to a festival cos of the toilet situation!! 😲

RedVelvet: loving your work, Hermione hahahaha

billythekid: 😄😄

Leothelionking: You made me laugh! Congrats!

(scroll down to see 29 more comments)

Chapter Ten: Lucy

After a busy morning of vlogging and checking out the scene, the gang regrouped in the VIP area. Lucy had enjoyed helping Abby out with her radio interviews, but now she was ready to enjoy some bands. She hadn't seen any live music since coming to the UK.

'There are s-so many different b-bands to choose from,' she said, looking at her programme. 'How are we going to d-decide? I mean apart from Ollie St-Storm.'

'There's this new girl band – the Daisy Deadheads,' said Sassy. 'They're down on the western stage in about an hour.'

'Cool,' said Abby. 'They might be wearing something amazing I could mention in my next fashion round-up. But all I really care about is seeing Ollie on the

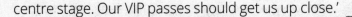

centre stage. Our VIP passes should get us up close.'

'Er . . . should I be jealous?' asked Charlie.

'Probably!' Abby laughed. 'He's gorgeous.'

'I'm s-sooo excited to see him in real life!' said Lucy. He'd had three UK top ten hits in the last year, and Lucy listened to his music all the time. She was obsessed with him on social media too – she followed him on Instagram and liked his photos almost immediately when he posted. He was sooo dreamy.

Suddenly there was a loud growling noise. 'Sorry, that was my stomach,' said Hermione, and they all laughed. 'What? I'm starving! Talking about all that nice food while I was filming made me hungry.'

'I could kill a hamburger,' said Jessie. 'Let's get some food while we're still in the posh bit.'

They headed for the VIP food trucks. Lucy had seen some delicious-looking tacos earlier and wandered off to find them.

The Mexican food stall was half hidden behind the henna-tattoo parlour, and when Lucy reached it, there was only a short queue. In front of her stood a young man with his back to her, holding a Siberian Husky on a lead.

'Oh, isn't she b-beautiful!' exclaimed Lucy, staring at the dog's snow-white snout and pale blue eyes. 'May I p-pet her?' she asked, and looked up at the owner and into the face of Ollie Storm.

She froze, trying to take this in. She – Lucy Lockwood – was standing next to the most famous pop star in the world. And he was smiling at her. And his smile was gorgeous.

'Sure,' he said. 'Just talk to her first so she knows you're a friend. Her name is Gigi.'

Of course! Now she realized she knew Gigi from Ollie's Instagram. Lucy could feel her heart beating really fast – could he hear it? She didn't know what to do. She just stood there, paralysed.

Ollie smiled at her again. 'Here, Gigi, meet a new friend,' he said, patting the dog.

What is wrong with me? Lucy screamed

inwardly. *Pull yourself together, girl!*

Slowly she stretched her hand out towards the dog and whispered, 'Gigi, you're a b-beauty. You have the m-most amazing eyes.' She stroked the dog for a few minutes while she composed herself, then she looked up. She knew her face was bright red, but there was nothing she could do about that.

Ollie was ordering his tacos and not paying attention to her, so she felt a bit calmer.

'Gigi seems to like you,' said Ollie a few moments later. 'You should feel honoured. She can be a bit picky about people. You must have a knack with animals.'

'I-I-I . . . I-I v-v-volunteer at an a-a-animal sh-sh-shelter,' Lucy stammered helplessly, her nerves overcoming her.

OMG. Why does this have to happen to me now? she thought. *Here I am with Ollie Storm, who is talking to me like I'm a normal person, and I'm behaving like a complete dork!*

'That sounds cool,' Ollie replied kindly. 'And what brings you here to Chesterbury? You're not rescuing animals here, are you?' He laughed.

'N-no . . . I'm h-here—' she started.

Suddenly she heard a familiar shrill voice. 'Lucy, darling!'

Dakota.

'Luce, I've been looking for you all over. Where did you get to?' Dakota said sweetly. 'I thought I'd lost you . . . my bestie.' She gave Lucy a big hug (Lucy nearly choked from Dakota's powerful vanilla perfume), then turned towards Ollie and gave him a radiant smile, while flicking her long, glossy hair.

'You naughty thing, Luce, keeping him all to yourself! What a lovely dog,' Dakota said, and lunged at Gigi, grabbing her fur. Gigi pulled back quickly and growled.

'Hey! Take it easy!' said Ollie to Dakota. 'She obviously doesn't feel comfortable with you. Or maybe it's your perfume. It's kind of . . . strong. Lucy, would you mind holding her while I get a drink?' He handed Lucy Gigi's lead and walked off, taco in hand.

Lucy stared after him, still in a trance, then turned to

Dakota and said, 'What are you d-doing?'

'Well, I saw you standing there making an utter fool of yourself, so I thought I'd step in. You should thank me. It was obvious you needed rescuing,' Dakota sneered.

Lucy was speechless. She couldn't really argue with that last bit.

Ollie returned. 'Right, girls. I've got to head off for a sound check. Thanks, Lucy, for looking after Gigi. You're a star. Hope you have a great day.' He took a bite of his taco.

'Wait!' said Dakota, holding up her phone. 'Would you mind if I took a selfie of us? It would be such an honour—'

'Sure thing. Lucy, budge up close to me so you don't get left out,' he said.

Lucy's heart skipped a beat. Dakota gave Lucy a poisonous smile and took a few selfies of the three of them.

'That's sooo kind!' Dakota oozed. 'I'm really looking forward to your set tonight. I've got a seat backstage.'

'Cool. OK, gotta split. See ya around,' Ollie said, and headed off with Gigi trotting alongside him.

'With a little editing, this is going up on my Insta,' Dakota announced, looking at the photo on her phone. 'Too bad you won't be in it!' She flounced off.

Lucy stood silently digesting what had just happened, a lump forming in her throat. She had met a world-famous pop star, who was not only handsome but kind, not to mention his beautiful dog. It was a dream come true. He had tried to strike up a conversation with her and she had made a complete hash of it. She might even have asked him for a short interview for the channel. What a missed opportunity; Abby would be furious when she heard. She hated her shyness and her stammer. She was such a loser . . . For once, Dakota was right.

'What took you so long?' asked Jessie, who was tucking into her hamburger with gusto. 'We thought we'd lost you. Hey, are you OK? You look kind of flushed.'

'You'll n-never b-believe it,' said Lucy. Still stammering more than usual, she filled them in.

'What?' shrieked Abby. 'The REAL Ollie Storm? Talked to you?'

'Yeah,' said Lucy quietly. 'But I r-really messed up. I d-didn't make the most of it, or even ask him if we could f-film him.'

'That would have been PERFECT.' Abby sighed.

'Don't worry, Lucy!' said Hermione firmly. 'Any one of us would have been dumbstruck in the circumstances – even you, Abby! Don't sweat it. Just enjoy the fact that you actually met Ollie Storm in person.'

'So cool!' agreed Sassy.

'Soz, Lucy,' said Abby, giving her a hug. 'I wasn't criticizing you.'

Suddenly Dakota came into view, vlogging herself as she walked.

'I'm so lucky to be a Diamond VIP here at Chesterbury.' She flashed her diamante wristband. 'I'm staying in this fabulous yurt, which has a hot tub and sauna. I have free use of all the beauty treatments and the blow bar, as you can see . . .' Dakota flicked her long hair. 'But best of all is having access to the backstage area. It means you get to meet all the bands and mingle with the stars.'

'Ugh!' Jessie burst out in disgust. 'She's at it again. How can one person be so infuriating? Just cos Daddy can buy her whatever she wants.'

'What's infuriating is that all that luxury is wasted on her!' said Abby angrily.

'Guys, I-let's just go I-listen to some music,' said Lucy, who was feeling too worn out to deal with Dakota again.

They joined Josh and Charlie and headed off to the western stage.

The next couple of hours were blissful. The Daisy Deadheads were awesome and Lucy enjoyed sitting on the grass in the warm sunshine listening to the band. She wished Sam were there, but apart from that, it was a pretty idyllic afternoon.

'It's a good thing I warned you all to bring sunscreen and sunglasses,' said Abby as the day hotted up.

'Abby's festival tips come good!' Sassy laughed.

They stretched out, talking lazily in between songs.

'Just going to f-fill up my water bottle,' said Lucy, when she had summoned up the energy to move.

She walked off to find the refilling station, humming to herself as she went. She was beginning to feel better about the whole Ollie incident. Until, just out of the corner of her eye, she could see a vision of a green spangled mermaid – unmistakably Dakota – coming out of a Portaloo. Lucy was about to turn and hide, but then she heard Dakota scream.

'Help!' Dakota shrieked. 'I just dropped my phone down the loo into all the muck. What do I do?'

The people standing around her sniggered and stood staring. No one made a move.

This cannot be happening, thought Lucy in amazement, wondering if she should get the others.

'It's a brand-new iPhone – the latest model – with a Swarovski case!' Dakota whined. 'I can't afford to lose it! There's a selfie with Ollie Storm on there! Arghh! These loos are SO badly designed; I'm going to get Daddy to sue the company that makes them!'

People started laughing. 'You'd better just dive in, love!' shouted a man.

'Eeew! It's so disgusting,' cried Dakota. 'Can't someone grab it for me?' She turned round and suddenly spied Lucy standing on the path nearby.

'Lucy! Lucy! Thank God. Come and help me!'

Lucy stood there, hysterical laughter bubbling up inside her. 'And why should I help you?' she asked. 'You're always absolutely foul to me. You treat me and my friends like dirt, and now you want favours! And you don't even say please!'

'Please,' pleaded Dakota feebly.

'I don't think so,' said Lucy firmly. She noticed with satisfaction that she wasn't stammering at all.

'Here's a coat hanger to help you fish it out,' said

someone from the crowd.

Lucy watched as Dakota went back into the cubicle and leaned down over the toilet bowl.

'Yuck, this is making me sick,' she whimpered, retching. The heat was making the bad smell stronger than ever. Dakota leaned over even more and suddenly lost her balance. She slipped into the opening, leaving both her legs kicking in the air.

Lucy gasped.

'Help! Help!' Dakota cried. 'I'm going to fall in!'

She sounded so pathetic that a couple of girls standing nearby grabbed her legs and tried to tug her out.

'Ow!' Dakota yelped, but she remained head down in the toilet.

The girls tugged her again, but she didn't move.

'I think you're stuck,' one of them pronounced as the crowd gasped and giggled in astonishment. Dakota's spangled right shoulder was firmly wedged in the toilet bowl.

'STUCK?' Dakota howled. 'I can't be!'

Lucy thought she heard a sob, and started to feel uncomfortable. It was a terrible predicament for anyone, even Dakota. She began to feel the weensiest bit sorry for her.

'Dakota, don't p-panic. I'll get help,' she said, WhatsApping the others.

In a few minutes the rest of the squad was on the scene.

'OMG!' exclaimed Abby. 'Here's a sight for sore eyes! There IS justice in this world.'

'Maybe we should film it?' suggested Jessie mischievously, but Hermione shook her head, and Lucy smiled in agreement.

'This is enough k-karma for one person, even Dakota!' Lucy said softly.

They all tried pulling out Dakota, but with no result. She was well and truly stuck, and Lucy could see she was getting increasingly distressed.

'I think we'll have to get h-help,' said Lucy. 'They might

have to d-dismantle the loo . . .'

Sassy went off to find a festival official and soon returned saying, 'They've called the fire brigade to rescue her!'

'Too bad Dakota doesn't have her vanilla spray to hand – it might help cover the stink!' commented Abby.

'Oh my God, guys, I've got a new name for her!' Jessie burst out. 'Poo-kota!'

It took a while for the fire brigade to come and a good half an hour for them to dismantle the loo and rescue Dakota. She looked and smelt terrible, and went back to her yurt to take a much-needed luxury shower. The phone was not retrieved.

After all the excitement, they got some more drinks and went over to the centre stage where the big acts were performing. You had to get there early to stake out a good position for later, and there were four acts lined up before Ollie Storm.

'Lucy, maybe you can walk around the stage and film

a bit of the scene to put in our vlog. You know, different angles and stuff, maybe a bit of backstage too, if you can sneak in. You're obviously a celeb magnet – you might meet someone else!' Abby said.

Lucy knew that Abby was trying to give her a chance to contribute to the vlog after the missed opportunity with Ollie earlier. And why not? She fancied a stroll. She filmed the crowds and then wandered back behind the stage where there were a lot of vans with technical equipment parked. There were also a couple of Airstream trailers, which were probably used as changing rooms for the artists.

Suddenly she heard a weak moan coming from one of them. It didn't sound human, more like an animal in distress. She peered through the tiny window of the trailer and could see a shape splayed on the floor. It was pale with some dark patches, and she could definitely see ears and a tail. Then she heard the faint whimper again. It had to be a sick dog.

She looked around for someone to help, but there

was no one to ask. Now what? She knew what she had to do. She opened the door of the trailer. It was like an oven inside – much hotter than out in the open. She rushed over to the dog and saw that it was Gigi. She was panting weakly and clearly having difficulty breathing. Saliva dripped out of her mouth.

'Oh, you p-poor girl,' exclaimed Lucy, her mind racing as she checked the dog over. 'You're overheating, but I'm h-here to help.'

Lucy picked up the almost lifeless body and carried Gigi outside. It wasn't easy, as she was heavy, but Lucy managed to lay her on the ground in the shade of the trailer.

'That's already a b-bit cooler,' said Lucy soothingly. Trying to think what her mother would do, she took the water from her water bottle and wet Gigi's tongue, paws and ears. The little water that was left, she poured gently on the back of the dog's neck. 'I'll just see if there's some more w-water inside the trailer,' she said, and soon emerged with a wet towel and a bowl of water.

She wiped Gigi down with the towel and gently coaxed her to drink. 'Come on, be a g-good girl and drink this up for me.'

Gigi's breathing sounded a bit more steady, but Lucy was still extremely worried – she knew that dogs could die of overheating. It happened when people left them in cars, and the trailer had been just as bad. Really what Gigi needed was a vet.

Lucy was on the phone to her mother when suddenly Ollie Storm appeared. He looked shocked and rushed over to Gigi.

'What happened?' he asked, his voice breaking.

'She overheated,' replied Lucy. 'It was like a f-furnace inside the trailer. I've just been t-trying to cool her down and get her to d-drink a bit.'

'But what happened to the aircon?' asked Ollie. 'I put her in there deliberately because it would keep her cool.' He got up angrily. 'Nothing works properly here. And the stagehand was meant to give her a bowl of water.'

Lucy stroked Gigi.

'Is she going to be all right?' Ollie asked anxiously, looking at Lucy.

'I think so,' replied Lucy. 'But I've asked my mother to c-come and have a look – she's a vet.'

'It would be a good idea to get her to an animal hospital and put her on a drip, just to be safe,' said Mrs Lockwood when she arrived a few minutes later. 'But I think she'll be OK. Lucy, you clearly acted quickly and did all the right things.'

'You mean she saved Gigi's life!' said Ollie emotionally. 'I can't thank you enough, Lucy. You're Gigi's guardian angel.'

Lucy felt a little bit of shyness creeping back in, now that Gigi was out of danger and she could go back to focusing on the fact that Ollie Storm was talking to her and saying he was indebted to her. This was the weirdest – and best – day of her life.

Later that night, Lucy and the gang all sat together at the

very front of the stage – which Ollie had arranged – and watched him do his set. The atmosphere was amazing: there were fireworks in the distance against the dark sky, and the audience all around them had sparklers or were using their phones to shine a light. It was magical.

And then, just as his set was drawing to a close, Lucy heard Ollie give her a shout-out from the stage and thank her for saving Gigi. The rest of the GCV crew couldn't believe it, and bundled her into a hug. The perfect end to a perfect day.

VLOG 9

Interview with Ollie Storm

13:48

FADE IN: VIP YURT – CHESTERBURY MUSIC FESTIVAL.

LUCY and OLLIE STORM are sitting opposite each other at a small table in a yurt at Chesterbury. Coffee and croissants are on the table.

LUCY

H-hi guys! So today I am th-thrilled and r-really honoured to be interviewing Ollie Storm in one of the g-green rooms at Chesterbury Festival. I've popped back specially! Ollie, I am really g-grateful you've given up your p-precious time.

OLLIE

Well, I'm grateful to you, Lucy, for saving Gigi's life yesterday, so I'm happy to help.

LUCY smiles nervously.

LUCY

OK, cool, let's get started! So my first question is about the f-festival. Have you enjoyed it?

OLLIE

Absolutely! I get such a buzz performing for an enthusiastic crowd, and I especially love outdoor festivals because they're more informal and friendly. It's so cool to share the love of

music with happy people in a natural setting. Did you like it
too?

LUCY is slightly stunned.

LUCY

Me? Oh yes. I mean, I've never been to Ch-Chesterbury, before
so for me it was awesome.

There is a nervous pause as LUCY looks at an index card on her
lap.

LUCY (CONTINUED)

So, Ollie, can you t-tell me a b-bit about your childhood and
growing up?

OLLIE

Sure! I grew up in the countryside. My mum's a teacher and
my dad's an engineer and I have three older sisters. They used

to tease me a lot, and I'd annoy them, but now we get along
really well. I did the usual things a kid does: riding my bike,
skateboarding, building huts in the woods – stuff like that.

LUCY

Did you have any p-pets?

OLLIE

Yeah, we always had cats and dogs,
and for a while I had a pet fox cub
that'd been injured and I looked
after. I love animals – as you do,
I know.

OLLIE smiles at LUCY.

LUCY

(blushing)

Guilty! And w-what about school? What's your b-best memory?

OLLIE

Mostly I liked school – apart from school dinners and some of the sports. I've always loved performing and I was always in the school plays. I'd say playing the lead in *Bugsy Malone* when I was about twelve was a highlight! I sang in the choir too.

LUCY

Cute. And your worst m-memory from school?

OLLIE

Being bullied, I guess. I got some grief because I liked music and drama. I learned how to stand up for myself, and it probably made me a stronger person overall. Loads of kids go through this stuff at school, but that doesn't make it any easier when it's happening to you.

LUCY nods earnestly.

LUCY

I'm sure loads of our viewers will r-relate. Now on to a l-lighter subject . . . What's your favourite food?

OLLIE

(grinning)

I'm currently obsessed with bangers and mash with loads of
onion gravy. And I wouldn't ever turn down a cheesecake.

LUCY

Nice. Your f-favourite movie?

OLLIE

That's tough. I'm a lifelong *Star Wars* fan, the original films
especially. But I have a real soft spot for *Finding Nemo* too.

LUCY

Ha! My little sister w-will love that. Favourite holiday?

OLLIE

That's easy. I went to Hawaii last year and learned to surf and
scuba dive. It's so beautiful there.

LUCY

Sounds amazing! W-what makes you happy?

OLLIE

Lots of things. A sunny day, hanging out with my close friends, a long walk with the dog, my family, a starry sky at night. A home-cooked meal.

LUCY

What is the closest to d-death you've ever been?

OLLIE

Yikes! Probably once when I was skiing. I stupidly went off-piste and ended up racing way too fast down a dangerous mountainside. Luckily, I managed to stop myself, but it was a real wake-up call to be more careful.

LUCY

Oh, I think we're g-going to have to wrap this up as I can see your manager is w-waving at me. Sorry to end on such a m-morbid question!

OLLIE takes a bite of croissant.

OLLIE

No problem, this has been really fun.

LUCY

One final question, then. What is your greatest w-weakness?

OLLIE

(laughing)

That's easy. I'm a hopeless romantic – and loads of things make me cry!

LUCY

Seriously? Wow, wish I could interrogate you f-further on that!

But it l-looks like you need to get to your n-next interview.

(to camera)

So a big thank you to Ollie Storm for allowing me to interview

him here at Ch-Chesterbury for the GCV channel.

OLLIE

It's been a pleasure, Lucy. Best of luck with your channel,

which gets a big thumbs-up from me!

FADE OUT LUCY and OLLIE talking.

Views: 436,559

Subscribers: 55,731

Comments:

Mgirlscanvlogfan: No way!!!!!!!!!!!!!!

MagicMorgan: Dead. Dead dead dead. RIP me.

ollienumberonefan: I'll dry your tears, Ollie ♥

ShyGirl1: Lucy, you're a natural! 👍

MrsOllieStorm: he's such a kewteeeeeeee marry me Ollie

StephSaysHi: Lucy I thought Sam was your bae

lucylocket [reply to StephSaysHi]: HE IS!!!! Ollie and I are just friends ;)

mia_vlogs: wow this is awesome xx

xxrainbowxx: Totes emosh!

girlscanvlogfan: 55K!!!!!!!!!!!!!!!!!!!!! Knew you could do it!!!!

Scroll down to see 13,024 more comments

Chapter Eleven: Sassy

12:02

Abby: OMG! Did you see Lucy is trending on Twitter?

12:02

Jessie: Whaaaa????

12:03

Sassy: It's a piece on how she saved the life of Ollie Storm's dog!

12:04

Hermione: Our very own celeb!!!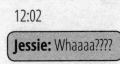

12:07

Jessie: Poo-kota must be sick with envy!

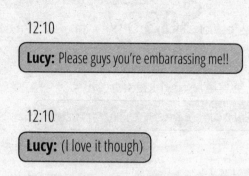

12:08

Abby: Go Lucy go Lucy go Lucy go

12:10

Lucy: Please guys you're embarrassing me!!

12:10

Lucy: (I love it though)

A week later Sassy was running up the stairs from the train station, while checking her phone. She was almost twenty minutes late because of a train delay.

'Sorry, sorry!' she called as she almost crashed into a mum with a pushchair coming down the stairs while WhatsApping the rest of the girls.

13:19

Sassy: Soz! Trains were crap! I'll be there in 5!

*

Ten minutes later she entered Pizza Planet, panting and a bit dishevelled. She spotted the others sitting at their favourite table in the corner.

'Hey, Sass!' Jessie called, and they all waved as she joined them. 'Grab a seat and we'll order some pizza. We're hashtag *starving*.'

'Sorry, everyone!' Sassy apologized as she sat down. 'It's so annoying living so far away from you all.' Hoping to speed things along, she beckoned the waitress over.

'Don't worry – we understand,' said Abby. 'We've just been gossiping and catching up. I can't believe it's been a week since we saw each other.'

'I know. I was so exhausted when I finally got home that I slept for, like, two whole days,' Sassy said with a grin. 'My bed felt soooo good.'

The waitress came over and they placed their orders.

'So,' continued Sassy, 'what's everyone been up to? And how is our very own celeb?'

'Stop it!' Lucy grinned. 'Well, I've been w-working flat

out at City Farm this week. I've been in charge of
the petting zoo and also h-helping out with some
of the activities for the little ones. Exhausting b-but fun.'

'What about Sam?' Sassy asked. She hadn't met Lucy's
boyfriend yet, but she'd seen him on some of her vlogs.

'He's been at the farm too. So that's b-been great.
We've managed to sp-spend a lot of time together to
make up for when we were apart.'

'Make up or make out?' Jessie teased.

Lucy blushed, and they all laughed.

'Luce, what did Sam think of the whole Ollie Storm
adventure and his shout-out to you at the gig?' Abby
asked, raising her eyebrows.

'What she means is: was he jealous?' Sassy said.

'No, of course not!' replied Lucy. 'Though I know
he wished he'd b-been there – it was such a special
moment.'

'Speaking of special moments,' said Abby
mischievously, 'how's it going with Leo, H? Has he been
in touch?'

Hermione smiled shyly. 'Ummm, we've been texting since we got back. Leo wants to come and see me soon.' She coughed nervously. 'But I'm due to go off on holiday with my dad next week, so I probably won't get to see him for ages.'

'Absence makes the heart grow fonder!' Jessie said.

'And what're you up to, Jessie? Any great pranks recently?' Sassy asked, reaching for a dough ball the second the waitress lowered the plate. 'I saw this really funny PeterPranks video yesterday and thought of you!'

'Trying the weird German sweets? I saw that too! Not so many pranks for me – I've got another gymnastics competition coming up, so I've been getting in training. I had a session this morning, probably why I'm so ravenous!'

The pizzas arrived, and they all tucked in.

'What's new with you, Sass?' asked Jessie.

'Well . . .' Sassy suddenly felt a bit flustered. 'I've been trying to finish the scary movie. It's quite hard cos we didn't get all the footage we'd planned, but I've been doing some cutting and editing, and adding in sound effects. It's actually coming together quite well. I could show it to you all later, if you guys want?'

'That sounds awesome,' said Abby, and Lucy nodded.

'I can't wait to see it,' said Hermione. 'It was such fun to make.'

'So much fun,' agreed Jessie. 'I've been telling my brothers how great it is – Leon loved the trailer and for once didn't diss our content!'

Sassy felt a wave of relief sweep through her. Ever since the 'incident' at the campsite, she'd felt ashamed of what had happened and unsure whether she'd really been forgiven for causing such a drama. Abby had reassured her a few times, but Sassy wasn't sure how the others felt. Everyone seemed fine about it today, though, even Lucy.

'So, who's coming back to mine after this?' asked Abby. 'I thought we could do a wrap-up vlog of the trip, with our favourite moments. And also some forward planning on where we want to take the

GCV channel. The festival viewing figures are amazing, especially the Ollie Storm interview. We've hit fifty-five thousand subscribers, guys!'

'That is IN-SANE!' exclaimed Sassy, her heart racing. She was so excited to be part of this channel and, more than that, she was excited to have made four good friends.

They finished their pizzas.

'I'm m-meeting Sam for a quick coffee, but then I'll come along to yours a b-bit later, Abs,' said Lucy.

'Wait – before you go, Luce. We've got a little something for your parents,' said Sassy, suddenly remembering the bag at her feet. 'It's a small thank you for the amazing holiday they so generously laid on. We all chipped in.' Sassy produced a large carrier bag with a flowering potted plant inside and handed it to Lucy.

'It was Sassy's idea,' said Abby.

'Oh, guys. That's so s-sweet. They'll be r-really thrilled,' Lucy said. 'Thanks, Sassy.'

*

Later that day, back at Abby's house, Sassy, Abby, Jessie and Hermione were sitting in the garden on sun loungers.

'I love summer!' exclaimed Jessie, painting her toenails a bright purple. 'I wish it would go on forever.'

'Me too!' agreed Abby, applying some sunscreen to her arms and legs. 'I've got factor thirty here for anyone who wants it. I hope Lucy comes soon so we can film out here in the sunlight.'

Just then they heard the doorbell, and Lucy came through the kitchen into the garden.

'Sorry I'm late. Let me c-catch my b-breath. I ran all the way,' panted Lucy.

She looked really frazzled, thought Sassy, hoping that nothing had gone wrong with Sam.

'Relax,' said Hermione, and handed Lucy a glass of lemonade.

'You look really weird,' said Jessie. 'Has something happened?'

'Yes!' said Lucy, breathing hard. 'You'll never b-believe

it, but Ollie S-Storm just called.'

'Shut. Up,' said Sassy.

'It's true! He's invited m-me and my family over to his p-place in the country so I can s-see Gigi again. He calls me her g-guardian angel.' Lucy grinned.

'A dog-mother instead of godmother,' joked Jessie.

'OMG!' exclaimed Abby. 'You're invited to his house? That's sick. Maybe you can do a vlog tour.'

'Abs! No! This is s-strictly p-private. I'm not filming there. It would be r-rude.'

'Oh well, maybe just a sneaky selfie?'

'Abby, you are shameless!' Sassy laughed.

'But that's why we love her,' said Hermione, and Sassy had to agree.

They sat in pleasant silence for a few moments, reflecting on Lucy's news, then Sassy had to speak her mind.

'You guys, I don't mean to sound soppy or anything, but I just wanna say that I'm so pleased to be part of the squad . . .' She had to stop because her voice was wavering.

'Aww, we love you too!' said Abby, and they all piled on top of her to give her a hug.

Sassy felt a bit embarrassed, but mainly just happy.

'So, Lucy – not even a short tour of his garden?' Abby continued. 'Or maybe the kitchen? Wait. What about the dog house? Lucy!'

VLOG 10

FADE IN: ABBY's GARDEN.

ABBY, LUCY, HERMIONE, JESSIE and SASSY are sitting in ABBY's garden, crammed on to a bench next to a little pond, drinking lemonade out of copper tumblers with stripy straws.

ABBY

Hey, everyone! So, now that we're back from our hashtag

amazing travels, we wanted to
look back and discuss the best,
and the worst, moments from our
trip. I made us these fancy drinks
so we could toast getting back in
one piece. Cheers!
They all clink glasses.

ALL
Cheers!

ABBY
OK, lots of reminiscing . . . Who wants to go first?

LUCY
M-me!

ABBY
Hm, I wonder what could possibly be YOUR best moment!

LUCY

Yes, yes, it was interviewing Ollie St-Storm. And, well, j-just meeting him! And Gigi. I still c-can't believe it all happened. It's the f-first thing I think about when I wake up every m-morning!

SASSY

We are definitely not jealous. AT ALL. Worst bit?

LUCY glances awkwardly at SASSY.

LUCY

Well . . . Sorry, Sass, but if I'm being honest, it's when you were missing on the l-lake. It was the worst few hours ever!

SASSY

I get that – sorry again. And, while we're on the subject, my worst one was getting stranded in that storm!

HERMIONE

Don't blame you. I think we would all pick that if it had
happened to us!

SASSY

I know, right? Anyway, on a more positive note, my best
moment was making the scary movie. You guys all worked with
me so well and I can't wait to show it to

(to camera)

YOU GUYS!

ABBY

You were amazing as the director – and hopefully we can make
more films together.

SASSY

We HAVE to! What about you, Abs?

ABBY

Well, obviously my WORST was Dakota getting up in my face

again – yes, you, Dakota, if you're watching, stealing my make-up ideas as usual! BEST was doing the fashion interviews at Chesterbury. So much fun and everyone was really lovely to talk to. H?

HERMIONE

(immediately)

Worst – mouse in tent. Or rat or whatever.

(shudders)

Best . . . was meeting new friends.

LUCY

(smiling)

Anyone in particular?

HERMIONE

Yes FINE. As you KNOW, I liked meeting Leo.

(blushes)

Hi, Leo, if you're watching.

ABBY

Cute! And finally you, Jess?

JESSIE

BEST – seeing Dakota stuck in the toilet, ha ha! And SUPing!

SASSY

And worst?

JESSIE

(quietly)

I guess . . . when things were weird between me and . . . one
of you. I don't want to tell the viewers, but we all know what I
mean, right? Anyway, just being honest! And we all know you're
not proper mates if you don't have a blazing row now and
again, to clear the air.

ABBY glances at JESSIE and smiles.

ABBY

Great answer, Jess! So, guys, that was our camping trip wrap-up. Now please enjoy this extra footage we haven't shown you yet . . . and see you soon!

They all wave, and a montage of the girls toasting marshmallows, laughing in the mud at Chesterbury, hiking through the woods, eating ice cream, and singing in the car plays.

FADE OUT.

Views: 27,569

Subscribers: 56,234

Comments:

girlscanvlogfan: absolute #squadgoals xxx

ShyGirl1: if I met Ollie Storm nothing in my life would ever top that!!

lucylockets [reply to ShyGirl1]: haha I knowww, that's what I'm worried about!

MagicMorgan: wish I'd been with you guys . . .

queen_dakota: What a sad little trip! Vermin in the tents . . . disgusting.

jazzyjessie [reply to queen_dakota]: some might say going phone-fishing in a huge vat of poo is disgusting

Scroll down to see 12,675 more comments

Top Ten Tips: So You Wanna Be a YouTuber?

Whether you're just starting out or are an experienced vlogger like the Girls Can Vlog crew, you may get stuck for ideas of what to film. YouTube trends come and go, but certain types of video are always popular.

If you need more tips on how to start a YouTube channel, read the 'Top Ten Tips' in *Lucy Locket: Online Disaster*, *Amazing Abby: Drama Queen*, *Hashtag Hermione: Wipeout!* and *Jazzy Jessie: Going for Gold*.

Please remember you need to be at least thirteen to set up a YouTube account.

So, without further ado, here are some ideas for fun and engaging content!

1) FASHION

One of the most popular types of video is anything to do with fashion. It could be focusing on one outfit for a special occasion – the clothes, shoes, accessories – or it could be a range of outfits for a trip or season – a 'look book'. Abby's fashion vlog at Chesterbury Festival is a good example.

2) MAKE-UP

Beauty tutorials are some of the most viewed videos on YouTube because they are so good at showing how to apply make-up and achieve a specific look. You can learn a lot from a make-up tutorial and they make fascinating viewing even if you aren't trying them out right then. Get Ready with Me is a good one, and you can keep it really relaxed and casual. You could do hairstyles too.

3) MORNING AND EVENING ROUTINES

These are fun videos that give viewers an insight into your life. They can include everything from brushing your teeth, doing your make-up and hair, getting dressed, exercises, what you eat for breakfast, walking the dog, to running a bath and setting your alarm last thing at night.

4) HAULS

Everyone loves to watch people 'unbox', whether it's presents at Christmas or birthdays, or packages they've bought in a shop or online. If you've been shopping for your summer wardrobe or for going back to school, you can unpack the shopping bags and talk through your purchases. Shopping hauls don't just have to be for clothes; they could be for make-up, stationery, books or decorations for your room . . .

5) BOOKTUBE

If you love books and reading, these videos will probably come quite naturally to you. Hermione does book reviews and book quizzes. You can also film your bookshelves if you have them arranged in a particularly creative way, or you could focus on your favourite book covers. Doing movie reviews is also fun.

6) ROOM TOURS

People love to get a peek into someone's bedroom or other rooms in their home. Many YouTubers do room tours and talk about their design ideas and where they got their knick-knacks. Do you have any interesting pictures or posters on your walls? It's a great motivation to start tidying up your room as well!

7) COOKING/BAKING DEMOS

Hermione loves to vlog her baking – whether it's everyday baking, such as cookies and cupcakes, or seasonal baking for Halloween or Christmas. Cooking demos are great fun too: for example how to make a fabulous pizza with all your favourite toppings; or how to make tacos, as Jessie did with her dad.

8) CHALLENGES

These are some of the most popular videos on YouTube. They can be physical-fitness challenges, such as yoga or gymnastics, or they can be more light-hearted, like popping balloons or trying not to laugh. Food challenges like the Chicken Nugget Challenge, which featured on the Prankingstein channel, are always hilarious. The Girls Can Vlog channel has featured lots of food challenges too: the Chubby Bunny Challenge, the Chili-eating Challenge, the Pancake Challenge and more!

9) Q&AS OR TRUTH OR DARE

There are hundreds of variations to these videos where you can quiz your friends or members of your family to let viewers get to know you better. Abby's Best Friend vs Boyfriend video is a fun example of this. Truth or Dare videos can be hilarious. Remember to prepare your questions in advance.

10) CHILD VS TEEN

These are fun skit videos where you act out the difference between how you might have reacted to an experience as a child versus how you are now. It's fun to dress up to make yourself look like a little kid for the child part and do silly things. You could use different voices. The more you exaggerate, the funnier it will be.

*

Hopefully these ideas will inspire you if you get stuck, but there are hundreds more out there – including ideas that haven't been dreamed up yet! Open your mind and get creative!

About the Author

Emma Moss loves books, cats and YouTube. In that order – though it's a close call. She is currently writing the next book in the Girls Can Vlog series.